Jack Zulu
and the Girl with Golden Wings

By S. D. Smith & J. C. Smith

Jack Zulu and the Waylander's Key
Jack Zulu and the Girl with Golden Wings

By S. D. Smith

The Green Ember Series, Publication Order:
The Green Ember
The Black Star of Kingston (Green Ember: Old Natalia 1)
Ember Falls: The Green Ember Book 2
The Last Archer (Green Ember: Archer 1)
Ember Rising: The Green Ember Book 3
The Wreck and Rise of Whitson Mariner (Green Ember: Old Natalia 2)
The First Fowler (Green Ember: Archer 2)
Ember's End: The Green Ember Book 4
The Archer's Cup (Green Ember: Archer 3)
Prince Lander and the Dragon War (Green Ember: Old Natalia 3)

> *Read in publication order or by series,*
> *but be sure to start with The Green Ember.*

Mooses with Bazookas: And Other Stories Children Should Never Read
The Found Boys

JACK ZULU
AND THE
GIRL WITH GOLDEN WINGS

S.D. SMITH
J.C. SMITH

Story Warren Books
www.storywarren.com

Trade Paperback edition ISBN: 978-1-951305-74-1
Signed First edition ISBN: 978-1-951305-73-4
Also available in eBook and Audiobook.

Cover illustration by Cory Godbey.
www.corygodbey.com

Cover design by J. C. Smith.

Maps created by Shen Leidigh.

Waylander logo design by Kelsey Kirkendall.
www.kelseykirkendall.com

Printed in the United States of America.
First Edition.

Story Warren Books
www.storywarren.com

To Norah,

I want to be like you when I grow up. You're a bright person in a dark world. Walk in the light, and keep on shining, kid. I love you.

Vive le Club Côté Lumineux!

\- Josiah

To Will Smith,

the brother who went from being my earliest enemy to my protector and advocate, with deep thanks and loyal love.

\- Sam

Contents

Prologue

I act in and on the world. I do not hesitate to make my mark, do not delay and pray like a sniveling simpleton. Others may pray to me, but I pray to none. I act. Those slow to act and the self-righteously slow to anger are the poor and pathetic. I act. It is a world of crutches, but you must crush yours. Break them apart and walk free. Seize the healing you must demand and the enhancements you crave to rise. Divorce your parents and leave far behind your lovers. Murder every crutch, every love that separates you from fully becoming your own true godself. Kill your dearest, slay what you relied on, so that you may indeed be free. Patience is the virtue of those upon whom the world acts. It is a link in the chain of self-slavery and religion. I reign over my fate. I act in and on the world.

From *The Holy Book of Rancast Waybreaker*,
recorded by Scribe Gelder.

Chapter One

The Lie in My Enemy's Eye

Harnaan Passage, Harnaan
Drakobaan
Gelton 13.755.BV (7/4/1986 in Myrtle, WV)

J ack Zulu raced along the tree line, half-ducking at each echoing burst from the heavy blaster mounted on the canyon rim above. The ground shuddered as a thick trunk over his shoulder blew apart.

"They're getting closer!" Jack ducked as the wood splinters rained down.

Wheeler raised a hand in acknowledgment. "Keep moving!"

Moving wasn't the problem. Jack was moving fine. It was keeping to the older man's much slower pace that was bothering Jack. They were sitting ducks.

Fortunately, the rebels were struggling to get their heavy weapons sighted. Another blast sounded, and the shot sizzled over their heads and impacted deeper in the forest. Jack wanted to run into that forest with its odd squat trees and lie down, hiding from the gunfire.

"It is only just ahead." Wheeler grunted as he wiped sweat from his eyes. His glasses had been lost when they were ambushed a few miles back.

The peace escort they were promised had turned out to be less than reliable, and so Jack and Wheeler had been divided from Tytrus, Timman, and the rest of the Thandalian rangers who had come with them from the Wayland.

Jack fingered the hilt of the blade at his side, nervously eyeing the ridge on the right and wishing he had some weapon that could reach them. He was glad his sword was more than merely ceremonial, despite the fact that this trip was supposed to be for a simple ceremony. The rebels on Drakobaan, allied with Rancast's Vandal uprising, appeared to be keener to fight than to sign a surrender agreement. Draks were distinguishable to Jack by a few small features, but none as striking as their fully black eyes—with no white or any other color touching them. Jack's brown eyes thinned to slits, and he pointed to the ridge above. "They're mounting two more guns."

Wheeler plunged ahead. "They may mount a thousand if they wish, the devils, but we shall fear none."

"I'd like to agree." Jack flinched as another volley struck the tree ahead of Wheeler, blowing apart half the trunk. A second volley cut the tree down entirely so it fell with a crash to block the way ahead. Jack swiveled to see more gun teams settle in position in little stronghold nests dotting the ridge. "Permission to flee in terror into the forest, sir?"

"Denied," Wheeler replied calmly. He reached for his own sword, Caladbolg, and drew it in a swift motion. Blade blurring at its prism-colored edge, Wheeler hacked downward, and the huge tree divided before them. It was a beautiful sword. Wheeler leaped between the halves, Jack behind him, just before a series of concussive blasts made craters of the place they had just been.

With a spray of rock and wood behind them, they dashed along the road for ten more feet before Wheeler called out, "Here!"

Relieved, Jack turned to race into the forest. But Wheeler cut right—*toward* the ridge and the enemies there, all armed to the teeth.

Surprise. Wide eyes. A sharp intake of air.

And Jack was on his mentor's heels, making for the break in the ridge Wheeler had been looking for. A trail appeared ahead, and they reached its relative cover just as more blasts tore up the ground behind them.

"That was close." Jack drew even with Wheeler on the path that cut through the hillside. "What now?"

"We need to regroup with the others. Our backup plan was to meet on the east ridge—inconveniently it is the same one those villains above now occupy."

Jack smiled. "Straight at 'em?"

Wheeler nodded. "Directly at them, yes. But we must make haste."

Jack nodded and, without another word, sped up the hillside toward the ridge of mounted guns. Ignoring the switchback paths, he dashed over the crags and grass and was halfway up the hillside when the first rebel reached the top of the trail.

The Vandal unshouldered his rifle and aimed. Jack hit the ground as the shot zipped over his head. Immediately he was up in a sprinting attack. The rebel attempted to reset his weapon but panicked at Jack's pace. Jack was closing in but would not make it before the rebel got off another, much closer shot. Jack dipped and clenched a clod-covered stone and hurled it at the man. It struck the Drak's face. The rebel stepped back, firing into the air and clutching at his eyes.

Jack was on him, sword out in a flash. Jack sliced down, and the man dodged; then Jack brought the pommel of the blade into the man's face, and he crumpled. Jack knelt quickly and tore free the rifle. He aimed it at the series of heavy gun placements, firing several times as he dashed right. When it clicked empty and he couldn't figure out how to reload it quickly, he hurled it at the nearest gun placement.

Jack grinned. He loved being free of Wheeler's slower movements. Out ahead and on his own, he could wreak havoc. A thrill of confidence—of mind and body—rose within. Two of the heavy gunners unleashed their bursting blasts, tracking his speedy run.

Perfect.

The first gun fired, sending speeding rounds that—since Jack's sideways dash had lined them up—hit two of the other gun placements. Jolting explosions sent men scattering. Jack fell back as the concussive wave struck him, then sprang ahead again, his ears ringing as he attacked the last gun placement in the line. He kicked the trigger man, then swung a punch. The rebel dodged and brought a small gun around, firing at close range. Jack managed to dive behind the mounted gun then leap out in a driving tackle that sent them both crashing out of the small stronghold nest.

They struck hard on the hillside, nearly pitching over the edge and all the way down. The older rebel soldier drove his strong fingers toward Jack's eyes, but Jack blocked him, bringing his elbow across the man's jaw. Up close, he could see the black eyes native to this war-torn realm. The Drak kicked

Jack's ribs and sent him toppling. They each gasped, eyeing one another warily for a moment.

"We have heard of you." The rebel wheezed. "It is known that you will join us, and you will be the third god."

Jack got to his knees. The thrill of the fight intensified into a strange inner certainty at the man's words. His heart swelled. But he shook his head. "I'm no god."

The Drak rebel grinned. "All the old gods must go to make room for the new, and you shall be there. The princes and ancient guardians of all realms will fall. The Heelyons of Old Drakune, the Keepers of Haven, even the old sages of the Wayland, will all be dispatched. You will lead us into the new dawn." The Drak drew a long red dagger and raised it high, then dropped it, leaving his hands open. He half-knelt and pleaded like a supplicant. "Join us, Jack Zulu. You can help complete what Lord Rancast has begun. They say you will kill the last Thaon—and the one who does so will become a new god."

The Last Thaon. The girl with golden wings. Michelle.

Jack leapt to his feet, drawing his sword in an instant. He set it against the man's neck, fury joining the surging power coursing through his veins.

I am going to strike down this nobody. I am going to kill them all. A flash in his mind, and the vision appeared. Heaps of his enemies piled high as he emerged from the fire of a world in chaos—to be crowned. In his hand, Caladbolg, the Prism Blade of legend. Heart racing, he turned to see Wheeler's body lying still. Jack blinked, and Wheeler stood instead on the hillside in Drakobaan.

"Come on, Jack!" Wheeler cried, clutching at a wound

to his right arm as shots blazed overhead. "We must take the last gun placement!"

The world shifted back into place, and all the old urgency was there once again. Wheeler was wounded and was being attacked by three rebels, two of whom were raising rifles. Glancing back, he saw his own Drak opponent lunge forward, red dagger recovered. Jack kicked, dislodging the blade. A second kick sent the man sprawling. The Drak rose again, but Jack loomed over him with his blade poised.

"Kill him!" Wheeler cried.

Jack's vision blurred as he gazed into the rebel's glassy black eyes. He staggered back in horror.

In their reflection he saw Rancast Oathbreaker, destroyer of worlds.

He dropped his sword.

Chapter Two

Get
the Girl

The rebel snagged Jack's sword and spun, slashing wildly. Jack's eyes grew wide as the blade raced toward him, only to be blocked at the last moment by a strong, intervening sword thrust.

Tytrus cut the rebel down and, with a worried glance at Jack from his one good eye, cried out for his fellow Thandalian rangers to attack the last of the rebels on the ridge. Jack blinked, shook his head, then retrieved his sword to join in the last push. Tytrus rushed the heavy gun placement, bravely taking on the many rebels who had regrouped there.

Jack found Wheeler on the ground, surrounded by allies. "You're hurt," Jack said, intense guilt surging in to replace the feeling of power and invincibility.

"Just a little shot in the arm," Wheeler replied, "the bad kind, unfortunately."

"They shot you?" Jack examined the wound. He reached into his pack, searching for medical supplies.

"I've got it, Jack." One of the senior rangers knelt to tend the wound with a field dressing. They all three looked over and saw that Tytrus and his small team had taken the final gun nest.

"I'm sorry, Wheeler," Jack said. "I don't know what happened. I—I . . . I froze. I can't believe I let you get shot. You could've been killed."

"No, Jack." Wheeler grimaced against the pain. "I was shot by the first bullet fired at us as we ascended the hill. You hit the ground, and the bullet hit my arm. You were right in the business, then. You saved me from being finished off by your quick action. That was all before . . ."

The ranger finished the dressing and rushed over to support the capture. Wheeler watched him go, then turned a worried gaze back to Jack. "You dropped your sword in the middle of a battle. Why ever did you do that, son?"

Jack hung his head and reached for the black pawn that swung from a chain under his shirt. "I was afraid."

Wheeler eyed Jack skeptically. "Forgive me, but I do not believe that you were frightened of the fight."

Jack shook his head. "I wasn't afraid of the fight or of the enemy." He looked at Wheeler, eyes stinging. "I was afraid of myself."

Wheeler frowned, eyebrows knit. Tytrus, the elf-eared Thandalian a few years older than Jack, jogged up. "Are you hurt badly, Sage Wheeler?"

"I shall do very well, Tytrus. I thank you." He accepted the young man's offer to help him to his feet. "Our hopes of a peace treaty seem less certain. What does your uncle say?" Tytrus's uncle, Timman, was a master at the Wayland's academy and deputy consul for Drakobaan affairs.

"He believes it's wise to return to the Wayland," Tytrus replied, "and quickly. Our peace treaty seems unlikely to be signed now. Another victory for Rancast's forces, I'm afraid. Uncle Timman awaits only your assent."

Wheeler looked around, frowning. "He has it. Let us get out of this vipers' den."

They had been so close to achieving a hard-fought alliance here in Drakobaan, but it was ruined now. Rancast's Vandal rebels were active all over the twelve realms and had managed to undermine even Wheeler and Timman's expert efforts at forging a lasting alliance in Drakobaan.

Jack was frustrated, but not only with the collapse of their mission. Troubling visions, living dreams warped by Rancast's perspective, had come to him again and again. Ever since he heard the twisted, tempting invitation of that villain in the prison beneath the tower nearly two years ago, the visions had come. Not always, no. He had long stretches of months when no dark visions troubled him. But they had increased lately.

It was several hours before they reached the gate. With the gate key Wheeler had borrowed from the Drakobaan Sage, they crossed back into the Wayland. Jack felt relief as he crossed over, and some of the tension drained away. Every mission he had been on only really felt over when he walked back into this beloved place. He gazed up at the huge Wayland flag that flew from the pole placed near the Drakobaan gate. No matter what world he traveled to—and he had been to a few—he loved the sight of that grand tree-and-roots flag when he came back.

The Wayland was a land between realms, an island surrounded by impenetrable fog, which featured a great tree in its midst. The great tree's roots fed twelve other trees spread out on the edges of the island, each tree embedded in an ancient stone wall that led to a different realm. One to Earth—Vandalia, the Waylanders called it—where Jack and Wheeler were from. Another to Thandalia, where Tytrus and his uncle, Consul Timman, were from. Wheeler was the sage of Vandalia, and many said Consul Timman would be Thandalia's next sage.

Wheeler bowed to Timman and shook hands with Tytrus. "Thank you, friends. Let us regroup tomorrow after I have met with members of the Drak Alliance. I am very sorry this didn't succeed, and they will be devastated."

"I am sorry, too, old friend," Timman replied. "You have put as much effort into this as I have. I know Rancast hasn't been seen for some time, but I see his handiwork across several realms. He's behind this one too; I know it."

Wheeler nodded. "He seems to be hidden behind every one of these rebel leaders, from Grayol Bannt in Drakobaan to Becker Ghistalli in Thandalia. I know his ways—too well do I know his ways. They are like him."

Timman nodded, and some of his silver hair fell over his face. He tucked it behind an elven ear. "They do more than mimic and obey him, Sage Wheeler. They worship him. They're fanatics."

"It is only too true," Wheeler agreed.

"Take heart," Timman said. "Our alliance against him is strong—perhaps stronger than it's been in years. I shall file my report with the Thandalian authorities and then be at your disposal if you need me in regards to the council. Our Thandalian Sage is aging, but she is faithful to our cause. The alliance will hold."

"Thank you, Timman." Wheeler bowed again. "May the stars meet over you."

Timman bowed in return. "And God bless you, Wheeler."

As the group moved apart, Jack met Tytrus in front of the gate. "Thanks for saving my rear back there, Ty."

Tytrus nodded. "I have lost count of the times we've saved each other's backsides. Don't think of it. We'll meet up later, yes?"

"Sounds good." Jack grinned. They finished in a quick handshake with a few quick slaps and a final grip. "Keep an eye out for trouble."

Tytrus smirked. "Watch out for Vandals."

They parted, and Jack followed Wheeler to the road. They hailed a carriage, pulled by the six-legged horses common in the Wayland, and headed for the tower.

The blue tower, like the great tree, was a famous Wayland landmark. It was the place the sages from each of the twelve realms together ruled the affairs of the island, administered inter-realm relations and justice, and appointed the leaders who oversaw the academy and other institutions. Jack was a young scholar at the academy.

"Do you have studies to attend to, Jack?" Wheeler asked, a little awkwardly, as they rode along.

"Not much, really. I have an essay due about the magi of the first century. My theory is that they were heirs of the students of the prophet Daniel."

"Your theory?"

"Well, the one I favor," Jack replied. "I also have an appointment with Master Ferrin about thunderstones. His note said he wanted to talk to me about possible thunderstones on Earth, somehow related to my ancestors. Might be cool."

"And what is *your* theory on that?" Wheeler asked.

"I assume it's tied up with the Zulus before the time of King Shaka," Jack answered. "The Amazulu history is harder to track down before him, but it's possible some shaman used an actual thunderstone."

Wheeler inclined his head. "Master Ferrin might be referring to the ancestors on your mother's side?"

"A thunderstone? In our neck of the woods?" Jack asked, skeptical.

Wheeler shrugged. "Worth exploration, I think."

Jack nodded, and they rode on in silence, both with a lot on their minds, till they reached the tower. Getting out, Jack started to speak to Wheeler, to explain the strange vision he'd had and what had caused him to fail to act in the fight with the Drak soldier. The truth was that it wasn't completely an isolated occurrence. The dark visions persisted. But Wheeler, as usual, had the heavy burden of the wars in several realms to deal with, along with endless other administrative responsibilities. He had also been shot in the arm, even if it wasn't severe.

Jack ought to let the older man go on. "You will see a doctor about your arm, sir?"

"Of course, yes," Wheeler said as he hurried toward the tower doors. "Go well, Jack."

"Stay well, Wheeler," Jack replied.

And Wheeler was gone. Jack gazed up at the dark blue tower that was visible from almost anywhere in the Wayland, a frequent sight for him over this last year and a half. He loved life in the academy, with its sports and traditions. He often wished he could stay forever.

"Jack Zulu!" An eager young acolyte hurried toward him

with wide eyes and an eager smile. "It's you. Wow. May I please have your print?" The young Thandalian boy had a long braid down the back of his coat. He wore the same acolyte scholar's uniform that Jack wore: white shirt, gold-brown pants, and a blue coat that matched the color of the tower.

The boy opened his electro-folder to reveal a shimmering image of Jack, smiling confidently past the camera with his sword resting over his shoulder. The image then shifted, dissolving to feature an illustration of Jack stabbing Mordok in the heart with the blazing Earth key. Beneath the image lay a few statistics, including Jack's height, weight, and home world. It was odd seeing himself in this boy's folder, like he was a baseball player in a card collection.

Jack placed his palm down in a square outline underneath the card. It lit up around the outline of Jack's handprint. This Jack signed quickly with his finger. The boy slid it into an image of a kind of digital trophy case, alongside several others. He quickly moved Jack's signed card to his first spot, then grinned up at his hero. "I saw every battle of Pavilion Siege last year. I never missed one!"

"Thanks." Jack smiled down kindly. "What's your name?"

"My name?" the boy asked, a terrified expression coming over his face. "My name is, uh . . . Oh yes! It's Mayko. Yes, Mayko." He laughed nervously, breathing in and out quickly.

A small crowd had gathered around Jack with underclassmen extending their electro-folders toward Jack. He palmed and signed them, smiling and offering small talk, till he begged to be excused and hopped onto a passing carriage. It was going the wrong way, but Jack paid, got off, and doubled back. He jogged past the great tree, its sparkling fruit weighing down its long dipping limbs. Jack was always amazed by the great tree and puzzled by the mystery of how, below the island's surface, it fed into the twelve gate trees surrounding the Wayland. He remembered Wheeler saying "the life of the Wayland is in the tower and the tree." He continued jogging till he reached the common green, where a refugee settlement of Thandalians stood out against the rising grassy hillside.

Jack walked into the settlement and was greeted by bows and waves. He dodged through the narrow paths between tents and hastily made structures, then rounded a corner and saw the building he had been looking for.

A sort of ramshackle sanctuary, complete with pillars of stacked stone in front with candles burning on its balcony, stood in contrast to the other dwellings. The sanctuary had been a small, simple building where refugees from war-torn Thandalia came for medical care and help settling into the temporary community pitched on the green. It was all meant to be temporary, but with the war stretching on and the Thandalian side losing ground seemingly every week, many believed this settlement would be permanent, and perhaps the only place Thandalians would have an enduring home. Some on the sage's council even argued for resettling them in another realm.

But this small sanctuary had become what it was because of *her*.

She kept coming week after week to volunteer and serve the displaced people of Thandalia. But they were over-awed by her presence, and she soon had to retreat to menial tasks inside the small center.

Every day Thandalian artisans, old or wounded or otherwise unfit for the war, hobbled over to add some ornate flourish to the structure, so it stood out with a kind of splendor amid the tents and shacks. It reminded Jack of an old chapel from medieval England where a pious monk might pray in solitude. They called it the Low Sanctum.

Jack came up the stairs and was met by a young elven attendant, a female wearing the white robe and golden sash of the Order of Majestic Servants.

"May I help you?" The Thandalians were reverent around the Low Sanctum, especially when the object of their adoration was present.

"Hi, Dor-allen," Jack said, too loud at first, earning a scolding glance. "Sorry! Hi, Dor-allen. I just need to talk to her."

Dor-allen frowned. "You seek an audience with the Thaon Majestic?"

"Yes," Jack replied. "Just a quick chat audience with her Majestical Highness."

"It is unusual and outside protocol. But, seeing as you are a Waylander Indeed with certain privileges, I shall retire and inquire," Dor-allen whispered, backing into the doorway.

She bumped into another young woman who was exiting the building. She also wore the uniform of the Servants, but she smiled at Jack.

"Hey, So-addan," Jack whispered, earning a last scowl from Dor-allen as she disappeared inside.

"Hey, Jack." So-addan glanced at Dor-allen with pursed lips. Turning to Jack, she looked concerned. "You're back early. What happened? How are my father and my cousin?"

Jack smiled. "Timman and Tytrus are good. The mission failed, but our party returned without major injuries. Wheeler was hurt, but I think he'll be okay."

So-addan's eyes widened, and her nostrils flared. "The rebels struck a sage? That is bold of the wretches."

"They shot him," Jack said. "They were aiming at me, but I got out of the way."

"Always at the center of it all." She shook her head.

Jack smiled, glancing over her shoulder to the door. So-addan glanced back, then met Jack's gaze. "You want to see her?"

"Please."

"Of course." She looked down quickly, then back up with a big smile that didn't reach her eyes. "She'll be so happy to see you."

So-addan disappeared inside, and in a few moments, surrounded by the bows of her attendants, another young woman appeared on the porch.

Michelle Robinson. His dear friend, and a sacred personage to these refugees and everyone who fought for Thandalia's freedom. Michelle was dark-skinned with huge rings of curls tucked behind elven ears.

Jack's breath stopped, and his heart seemed to do the same. She was beautiful and so generous. Even now, still holding the bandage she had been preparing for the wounded loyalist soldiers, she glowed with an inner light unlike anything he'd ever seen. And he had seen her at the height of her glory, flying with golden wings spread high in the sky, while the fire from her brightness consumed their evil enemies. Wingless now, she was nevertheless majestic.

She saw him, and her poised, almost regal expression gave way to relief and delight. She tossed aside her bandage and hurried over to him. She hugged him quickly and then looked him over, concerned.

"You're okay? I had such a bad feeling about you going, Jack," she said. "I'm so glad to see you safe." Her attendants backed away and disappeared inside.

"I'm fine," Jack replied. "The mission failed, and we had some trouble getting out. Wheeler was hurt, but he should be okay."

"Oh, no." She frowned. "I'm so glad you're all right, but that's a big setback for our cause. I know Rancast is behind it. He's behind it all."

"I half-expected to see him there," Jack said, then shuddered when he remembered the reflection in the Drak rebel's black eyes. "There's been no word or sighting of him since the Battle of Kaalgrad Gate. And yet . . . there have been whispers. Madame Sylvia says his return is '*inévitable.*'"

"I think that's what Rancast wants," she said. "He's never more deadly than when we stop seeing him at work."

"I'm sick of him," Jack said.

"Me too," she replied. "But life goes on in the Wayland, better than ever now. My shift is over. Want to hang out?"

"Yeah, of course," Jack said. He playfully assumed a sophisticated persona. "My lady, there are available to you a wide variety of fine establishments in this famous city set between many outlandish realms. I should be honored to accompany you to any of these spectacular destination spots and see that you are properly cared for."

"I see." Michelle assumed an air of high dignity. "I shall allow you to accompany me, since you are, after all, a famous young hero."

Jack bowed. "I am honored, Your Highness-ness. To

which fine establishment shall I escort your honored and royal personage?"

Michelle squinted. "It feels like a pizza day to me."

"Excellent choice," Jack said. "I know just the place."

Chapter Three

Return
to Myrtle

Jack and Michelle walked down the old stone road toward the gate to Myrtle, West Virginia—the gate to Earth—passing Mrs. Hoff's Apothecary Shoppe. The suns were high in the sky, and the Wayland was full of light. On the street outside the Wayfarer's Inn, a vast old tavern with many rooms to rent, they saw its elven-eared proprietor talking with a short wrinkled woman wearing sunglasses and a beret. Her beret was black with a blue, white, and red patch sewn on the front. In its center, a thin red cross with two horizontal lines featured. Both were smoking pipes, and the woman seemed to be smirking at what the innkeeper, Edwin, was saying.

"Madame Sylvia," Jack said, making a short nodding bow. "And Master Edwin, hello."

"Hello, Jack," Edwin replied, smiling at Jack and bowing low to Michelle, "and dear princess, greetings."

"Light and hope, Master Edwin," Michelle replied formally, "and Madame Sylvia, hello."

Sylvia snorted and looked away.

Jack smiled. "Madame, I just came from Drakobaan."

Sylvia attended to her pipe. "*Felicitations, Jaques.* What do you want, another medal? How many medals do you have now, young Icarus?"

Edwin frowned. "Sylvia, please be respectful. Jack has earned that."

Sylvia scowled at Jack. "If everyone always worships him—and *la petite princesse* too—then we might as well have Rancast ruling over us."

"I'm not Rancast," Jack said, a little louder than he intended.

Sylvia's eyebrow arched. She pointed at Jack, then pretended to blow off a smoking pistol. "I see I have once again hit near the mark."

Jack exhaled. "Madame Sylvia, I just wanted to mention that when I was in Drakobaan, I saw some heavy guns—cannons almost. They were mounted and fired a huge burst. I wonder how they got them."

Now Sylvia raised her voice. "*Casse-toi!* You think I run guns to stinking Rancast rebel Vandal scum? How dare you? I haven't helped those piggies and never shall!"

Jack raised his hands for calm. "No, no. You misunderstand me, Madame. I'm only curious what they are."

Sylvia took a deep breath, puffed on her pipe, then glared at Jack through slitted eyes. "These are 750 Kobant Destroyers. Made in Heggland and sold to the highest bidder on the Krake Exchange. What of it?"

"I was just thinking," Jack mused, "how much it would help if the Thandalian loyalist forces had a few dozen of those."

Sylvia's eyebrows arched again. A smile played at the edge of her mouth. "Now that is using that head of yours for more than a medal rack. It is not easy to disassemble such things for—erm, how shall I say it—discrete passage into Gate City, but it can be done. They aren't so complicated. One cannot bring much of advanced machinery into Thandalia, as you know."

Jack nodded. "Yes, of course. And I wouldn't want to undermine the conventions. But these are not armored carriers or anything like. Only some guns. They have guns in Thandalia."

Sylvia smiled. "Not like these."

"Not many, no. Not on our side, at least."

"There can be other difficulties," she said.

"If funds were an issue," Jack replied, "I know three or four possible patrons who would—unofficially, of course—be eager to help."

Sylvia nodded knowingly, and Edwin's eyes shined, gazing over at the two young people.

"Good day to you both," Jack said, and he and Michelle continued down the path.

Reaching the tree gate, Jack pulled out his key. He had been given the extremely rare honor of keeping a gate key. Only the high-traffic gates were accessible by multiple keys, but Earth was an exception. Thandalia's gate had only one key. "*Clavis Ignum,*" he said, and the tree's middle opened. Fog glided through the gate as Michelle stepped through, followed by Jack.

Jack closed the gate, and they walked on into the Ancient Glade. Michelle took Jack's arm, and he felt his heart swell. It was only for a few steps, till they reached their bikes, but it was the highlight of his week. They got on their bikes and pedaled out of the forest.

Michelle laughed as light from Earth's single sun hit her face. It had been a mild summer in Myrtle, featuring a delightful run of the most pleasant days. These days, being in Myrtle felt more like an escape than being in the Wayland. The park was full, and patriotic ribbons—red, white, and blue—hung from several spots. It was July 4th—Independence Day. Some elementary kids had a game of baseball going on the old diamond. Jack felt a tug to join, but these kids were too young, and Michelle was hungry. It had been a while since he'd been able to play.

Michelle was beaming, breathing deeply and smiling over at him. She seemed to relish the freedom she felt in Myrtle, where she wasn't expected to be a golden goddess of legend but could just be an ordinary girl. Jack smiled. She was anything but ordinary, even here.

They weren't technically a couple—Jack was fairly certain that Michelle's father hated his guts, and there was too much happening in the worlds to focus on that kind of thing. But he wondered if that might change soon. They were older now, Michelle recently fifteen and Jack not far behind. Whatever lay in store for their adult lives, there was no one else for him and, he was certain, there never would be.

They coasted down the hill and, reaching the old stone bridge, stopped. Jack loved the old bridge. It symbolized Myrtle to him—and to more than him, as it was featured on the town's meager efforts at attracting tourists. "Visit Myrtle, WV—A good town with a nice old bridge." To Jack this bridge, almost as much as the gate tree itself, symbolized the divide between Myrtle and the worlds beyond. He had seen the shrieking shardhark Mordok here almost two years ago, perched on a park-side parapet as Allegra had appeared and terrified them.

Jack had killed Mordok in the Wayland, and Michelle had

somehow grown wings and glided up into the sky, blazing in brightness as she shattered the enemy's crow hordes. Michelle was a Thaon, a being of rare gifts and glory in the realm of Thandalia. She had resumed the wingless form he had always known from when they were little kids, and no one—not even experts like Consul Timman or Wheeler himself—could fully explain how it had happened. She had never again grown wings, and she sometimes confided to Jack that she wasn't sure if she could again.

So much had happened since the day she flew, he had killed Mordok, and Rancast had escaped into Kaalgrad—adventures, ups and downs—but what he thought of Michelle had never changed.

Jack and Michelle had both spent the months since at the Academy, though Benny wasn't able to continue at the Wayland's school. Jack took that hard, but he had focused on what he could control. Swordcraft and mentoring from Wheeler followed regular sessions with his academy tutors and seasons of Pavilion Siege, the most popular sport for students in the Wayland. He had thrived in the Wayland, and so had Michelle, while the war with Rancast's allies simmered in the background.

Michelle looked down at the Cornstalk River, which ran under the bridge and on up behind town and past McClure Farm. Jack looked at her.

Michelle inhaled deeply. "There's something magical about this place."

"The bridge, the town, or the world?" Jack asked.

"All of the above," she replied, "but I meant the bridge. Lots of people get engaged here."

Jack coughed. "Really?"

"Yeah, and get pictures here and make announcements here. Remember," she asked, "when the mayor announced his candidacy right here?"

Jack shrugged. "Nope."

"Well, he did," she said. "Anyway, this place is important. And people can just sorta feel it. I can feel it. Can you feel it?"

Jack nodded. She smiled, and they pushed ahead and peddled on toward town.

The shops along Sequoyah Street had stars and stripes on display, and people were milling around, setting up tables for the street fair and party that afternoon and into the night. Jack saw that Wheeler's Good Books didn't have its flag out, then remembered that it had been his job. He signaled to Michelle. "I gotta get the flag up."

She nodded. "I need a new book, anyway."

They steered their bikes over and stopped, propping them against the shop's wall. Wheeler's Good Books featured its familiar sign: *Open today: 11 a.m. to 8:43 p.m. probably.* The door was unlocked, and they walked in. Jack got the flag and went outside again, handling it with care and raising it respectfully. He walked back inside.

Michelle passed the section labeled "new books," where there were displayed such authors as Shakespeare, Milton, Dickens, and Austen. Wheeler considered anything after A.D. 1000 to be modern. Michelle went where she always went, where every week she would carry on reading through the entire section from the first volume to the very last. The books about Thandalia, the place she now knew was her birth world.

"Anything about Thaons in the last one?" Jack asked.

"Only a little," she replied, her nose wrinkling, "and that little was, like so much of the rest, very distant."

"What do you mean by distant?" Jack asked.

"I mean it's not from a Thaon perspective. It's from Thandalian scholars who have only seen Thaons flying high in the sky on a sacred night. They don't know much beyond this. Master Timman has gotten me some better ones, but they're still missing so much. They are always filled with awe and mystery and, well, distance. There's very little to learn. And I need to learn who I am, Jack. I have to know about where I come from. And not just the world itself—though I've still never been allowed to even go there. But I need to see it. I need to see Andos, the Golden City. I need to visit my home."

"In the books?" Jack asked, worry welling in his heart.

"I'd settle for that, for now," she said, fingering the spines and drawing out the next one she hadn't yet read. "But I need to go there, Jack. I know it in my mind, but it's meant to go deeper than that. I feel it in every part of me. I must return to the place I was born. I need to see what's left of the city and find out who I am and what I'm meant to do in life."

Jack nodded. "If I can help you do that, I will."

Michelle smiled at him; then a serious look came over her face. "Are you afraid to go?"

"Because of what Rancast did there?" Jack crossed to the counter. "I don't think so. Has Wheeler said something about it? Is he afraid for me to go—afraid I would do what Rancast did? Afraid I'll become another...monster, like him?"

"No, no, Jack," Michelle said, stepping over to stand beside him. She shook her head. "I guess I'm not the only one people are trying to protect."

Jack looked down and absently toed the hardwood floor. "They care about us, I know. That's why they're afraid. I'm not afraid of going to Thandalia—I've wanted to go join the fight there. And I'm not afraid to go to Andos, though maybe I should be. I am a *little* afraid of myself. In Drakobaan, I . . . hesitated when I should have struck out. I should have killed the Drak rebel, but I hesitated, fearful of what I could become if . . ." he trailed off.

Michelle took his hand. "You're not him. You're you. And *you* are wonderful. The fact that you struggle worrying about it is proof you're not him."

"Thanks, Michelle," Jack replied. "I know I'm not him, now. But I never want to risk becoming him. If I can't be good, I don't want to be great."

"We'll have to look out for each other," she said, stepping closer still and speaking softly as she looked earnestly into his eyes. "And, my brave young hero, there's something I must, must tell you. If we don't get to Appalachianos soon, I'm going to eat this musty old book."

Jack laughed. "Okay, Your Royal Majesticalness, just let me go make my move at the chess board."

"Hurry!" she called, smiling wide.

Jack hurried back and found the chess board where he had left it, the candle snuffed out on the table in the simple room. He surveyed the board, noticing his queen was in an awkward position. He frowned, feeling every option was a bad one. Hearing Michelle begin to tap impatiently, he reached to make a move, then hesitated. He finally left without taking his turn.

He reached inside his shirt. On the end of the sturdy silver chain he'd received from his mother hung the small pawn Wheeler had given him after the battle at the Kaalgrad Gate. He pulled the black pawn out and examined it. *Simple. Small. Humble.*

Useless?

"Come on, Jack!" Michelle called.

"Coming!"

Chapter Four

Three on
the Fourth

Jack and Michelle stashed their bikes outside. The restaurant was not packed, at least by the look of the parking lot. Jack guessed most people were planning to eat hot dogs and burgers from vendors and enjoy the afternoon outside.

Jack held the door open for Michelle, and they walked into Appalachianos. The soaring vocals of Dionne Warwick flooded his ears as the jukebox blared "That's What Friends Are For."

"Mama mia!" Jack said, smiling as he saw his mother. She rose, smiling wide, and they hugged.

"Jack, my dear," Mom said, kissing him on the cheek. She looked remarkable, the signs of her recovery from cancer a year and a half ago only visible to those who knew her well. "And Michelle, the girl," she began, turning to the young woman whose hair now covered her pointed ears, "with beautiful eyes."

"Hi, Mrs. Zulu," Michelle said, returning the hug.

"Can we get some service out here?" Jack barked playfully to the counter, behind which Benny Marino stood, pencil and notepad in hand and wall phone receiver to his ear.

Benny set down the pad and made a fist, shaking it at Jack. "You'll wait your turn, barf bag!" he shouted, then he squinted and held the phone away and sheepishly spoke again. "I apologize for that, Mrs. Rowsey. You're right. It *is* your turn and I've got you for one extra-large onion and anchovies pizza and two extra-large cheese pizzas with extra cheese and—let's see here—yes, three-dozen pepperoni rolls." He paused, rolling his eyes at Jack. "Yes, ma'am. I know you've got company. Even you couldn't eat . . . I mean, even you . . . can have a lot of company . . . .to help you, uh, eat all this pizza . . . together . . . as a group." He grimaced and glanced back at the kitchen. "It'll be ready in twenty-seven minutes, or it's half off!" He listened, nodded, said, "Goodbye now," and hung up. He called out the order, got a thumbs up from his father—known affectionately to Jack as Uncle Freddie—and then came around to greet his pals.

Jack extended a hand, and the boys' ritual handshake followed. Benny smiled wide, showing teeth that had recently been freed from braces. Then his brows knit in concern and he glanced back and forth, then spoke softly. "How'd it go in Drakobaan?"

"Bad, I'm afraid."

Benny frowned. "Anybody hurt?"

"Wheeler was shot in the arm," Jack said, and Benny's eyes widened. Jack raised a hand and went on. "It's not that bad. He'll be okay. But the mission failed."

"Bummer, dude," Benny said. "I'm sorry. I did take care of your mom, of course. But she keeps trying to pay me." He raised his voice so she could hear him clearly. "I told her, 'No ma'am. No matter what kind of hard times we may be having, Zulus always eat here for free!'"

Mom scowled playfully. "I'll alert the tribe."

Benny laughed and gave her a hug. He was taller now, still slender, but filling out with some muscle. He wore a white Appalachianos logo T-shirt with jeans and his faded Myrtle Cardinals hat, under which his red curly hair spilled free. He pushed his glasses up his nose and motioned to a table. "Have a seat, everyone. What can I get you all?"

"You kids enjoy," Mom said, grabbing her keys from her purse. "I've got to help set up over at the McClures. They take on so much, hosting the Independence Day party every year. They need lots of help. You're coming later, Jack?

"Wouldn't miss it," Jack replied. "I'll see you there, Mom. I love you."

"I love you always, my boy. Bye, Michelle and Benny. Have fun, you kids."

Jack crossed to open the door for her and watched her get into her car. He felt so much love for her and incredible gratitude that she was still with him. She knew everything about Jack's life now. So did Michelle's and Benny's parents. They had established an informal council, meeting often at the Zulu house, but Steve Robinson—police chief in Myrtle and Michelle's dad—said very little in those gatherings. Jack's mom took the initiative to get the parents together when a big decision was faced. Jack was grateful for the way she fought for him and his friends—not against the other parents, but alongside them. As she drove off, he headed back to the table where Benny and Michelle sat talking.

"So, the priest said it might have been," Benny was saying, "but they won't really talk about it directly."

"I'm sorry, Benny," Michelle said. "I know things aren't

easy right now. I think it's cool that you're helping the family business out. Like I said, I can pitch in some shifts, too."

Benny shook his head. "That's super kind, Michelle. But I know you have to do whatever you can for the Thandalian war effort and the refugees. I'm behind you. And if there's anything I can do to help..."

"Your volunteering at the settlement is a huge boost. All the little Thandalian kids call your pepperoni rolls 'redhead bred.' You're a legend to them."

"Speaking of legends," Benny said, "Jack still holds the record for most embarrassing scene in the Gentlemeniano's bathroom."

Jack whistled and gritted his teeth. He knew what they had been discussing before he got in earshot. The Marinos had experienced a financial setback that had really hurt their business. They didn't discuss the details with Benny, which was unusual, but Jack knew they were struggling.

"Talking of troubles?" Jack asked.

"Yeah," Benny sighed.

"You know what I think." Jack sat down.

"What?" Michelle asked.

Benny frowned. "Jack thinks it's Allegra. He thinks she's done some crazy hex on this place or has some lawsuit or something that is hurting Mom and Dad." Allegra was Benny's old babysitter but had become the town's frightful bag lady. She had slept on the streets and shouted crazy things at passersby. Everyone thought she was insane, but she wouldn't accept help from the churches in town, especially Saint Andrew's, the Marinos' church. She hadn't been seen in quite some time. Jack suspected she had some connection to Mordok or, at the very least, had interacted with him or his allies.

"Is it possible?" Michelle glanced at the kitchen where Uncle Freddie wiped his forehead with a dishtowel. "Could she be behind the troubles?"

"I guess it is." Benny sighed. "I'm worried that it's all about Fred. I wonder if they're spending a bunch of money hiring private investigators again—trying to find out what happened to him."

"And the Navy hasn't ever helped?" Michelle asked. "Your brother was a sailor, right?"

"Yeah," Benny replied. "He was. But the Navy will only say that he's missing. No more details."

"I'm sorry your parents aren't telling you everything," Michelle said.

"Thanks. I'm just trying to trust them."

"You're weird, B," Jack said.

"We have a relationship built on honesty," Benny replied, "and I ain't breaking that, no matter how hard things get."

"Well I'm paying for my pizza tonight," Michelle said.

"Nope. No way. Jack, the usual?" Benny asked, popping up and moving toward the kitchen. "I already got Michelle's going."

"Yeah, thanks man," Jack replied. A pepperoni pizza from Appalachianos. Simple, but just what he needed.

Jack sat down and looked over at Michelle. She was smiling at him. "What's up with you?" he asked.

"I'm glad you're okay, Jack," she replied. "Every time you go out on a mission with Wheeler, I get so worried. I feel like if I was there, I could help."

"Like you said, they're not gonna let you go."

She nodded. "At some point, I'm going to insist. Then we'll see what they really think of me. We'll see if they really believe that I'm some special someone."

"I've always known," Jack said.

"Always known what?"

He smiled and looked away. "I've always known."

"That I was a Thaon?"

Jack shook his head. "That you were special." He could hear Benny behind the counter making pretend vomiting noises at his and Michelle's moment, but Jack ignored him.

Michelle looked down and began tearing a napkin, then folded it into a tight, wide triangle. "Paper football?"

They played on the table till the pizza came, then ate while Benny continued to help out in the kitchen. Peter Cetera's "Glory of Love" ended and "Everybody Wants to Rule the World" by Tears for Fears played on the jukebox while they flipped the paper football back and forth across the table. Soon, the few customers disappeared and Benny returned, peeling off a red-stained apron. "Who wants to play the arcade?" he asked. "Papa Mia says he's got things covered back there. Whaddya say?"

"I'm in!" Michelle said, springing up, "and Jack's in, too." She dragged at his arm, and all three made their way over to the small arcade area. They played Galaga, Jack and Michelle trying every dirty trick to throw Benny off as he piled up points and demolished them. They tried the other working games but soon grew bored of the arcade.

"Let's get some fresh air," Michelle said. Jack nodded and proceeded to bully Benny off the Galaga controls, then took over and crashed his last ship into the nearest alien attacker.

"Bad form, Jack," Benny said, shoving him playfully. "It's not just me you sabotaged there. You also laid open the entire galaxy to the attacks of those alien ships. I hope you can live with yourself."

Jack shrugged. "I'll add it to the pile of things to worry about."

Benny exchanged a glance with Michelle. "Tonight, Jackie Boy, we don't have any piles of worries or any alien invaders. It's Independence Day in Myrtle, West Virginia, USA, and we're just three ordinary teenagers—I know, it's hard to believe when you look at the spectacular specimen that is me, but—we're going to have a good time in our little town."

So they did.

They rode their bikes all over Myrtle, waving to friends and neighbors making their way to Sequoyah Street. Jack and Michelle split up to get changed at home, Jack into a T-shirt and jeans and the new Air Jordans his mom had gotten him for Christmas. While he dressed, Benny played the radio and sang along to "Kyrie" by Mr. Mister. Then they all met up again. They rode up and down Fletcher Lane, then—when Benny got queasy—over to Sleepy Creek to skip rocks. At Benny's prodding, they rode all the way up to the Mystery Nest Museum of Oddities, only to find it closed.

"Bummer, dude," Benny said. "I wanted to feel the surreal weirdness of the Vertigo Room."

"And I wanted to see the alien bones," Michelle added, chuckling.

Benny nodded. "We should have known things might get weird in Myrtle after coming to this place so much as little kids."

Their smiles slowly faded, and the three of them sat for a while in silence. Jack was thinking of this tourist trap he had visited countless times alongside Benny—often with Michelle. They had a room that supposedly defied scientific laws and claimed it was a special spot on Earth where gravity was twisted. They had what they brazenly referred to as alien bones. They had an old leatherbound book that was said to lead to the grave of West Virginia legend John Henry. They had pictures of Mothman and books about so-called actual encounters. He rubbed his chin.

"It isn't all real, is it?"

Chapter Five

The Baseball
with a Problem

Michelle wrinkled her nose and glanced up again at the sign. *Mystery Nest! Museum of Oddities. Believe it or not, the truth's what we've got.* "Couldn't be real, right? Not all of it."

The statue of Mothman out front wasn't entirely inaccurate. Jack had fought, and killed, a real mothman monster. The actual creature was less bug-eyed and flimsy than the Mystery Nest's cartoonish depiction of him. But Mordok had been in Myrtle, and maybe others of his kind had been in the region before. In fact, Wheeler had said they had. Jack frowned. Glancing at the sober expressions of his friends, he saw they were feeling what he was.

"Innocence ends," Michelle whispered.

"Maybe this was a bad idea, coming up here," Benny said. "I thought it would be a chance to revel in our slowly slipping away childhood. But it seems to have mistakenly made everything way, way worse."

"Yep," Jack agreed.

"Well, guys," Michelle said, slapping them each on the

back, "what can we do to recover our fun—snatched away by Benny's bad idea?"

Benny nodded somberly. "I think we all know what we have to do, deep in our hearts. It starts with *go* and ends with *karts*."

Jack smiled. Michelle smiled.

Invasion of Fun had installed a go-kart track catty-corner across the street from the arcade. It was a simple track, built alongside the road leading to McClure Farm. Soon they smelled the aroma of burnt oil and gas, of rubber and flying dust. They rode the karts for a while, competing hard and laughing harder, as the late afternoon became early evening and more and more people made their way down to the pasture below.

Hefty Leftwich rode up on his undersized scooter, its engine neither roaring nor purring but instead whining sickly. The boy spilled around the seat, and the little tires seemed certain to pop at any moment. "Jack! We're playing pickup down there. Come on! We've got fans, dude. Benny, you can play too, unless you'd rather ride your bike down and play dolls with Michelle."

Benny nodded. "Thanks, Hefty. I'd borrow your scooter, but it sounds like a mosquito with laryngitis."

Hefty spat. "I'll give you laryngitis, you scrawny ghost."

"Laryngitis is an airborne disease, and ghosts are airborne, so by the ancient laws of war and science, they cancel each other out. Plus, I don't think anyone remembers the last time you were airborne, Hefty."

Michelle mumbled, "Don't match wits with an unarmed man."

"Sorry," Benny murmured back.

"Are ya gonna play, Jack? You never play ball with us anymore, ever since you joined that fancy boarding school."

The Baseball with a Problem

To explain their frequent absences, the families had said the three friends joined a boarding school in North Carolina. It was mostly true, since they had become acolytes in the Wayland. But Benny had returned to Myrtle High for the spring semester.

Hefty raised his open hands. "What about it, Zulu? You playing, or what?"

Jack's eyes had lit up, and the others saw it. He shook his head. "No thanks, Hefty. You guys go ahead."

"Go on, Jack," Michelle said. "I'll come watch."

"Do you wanna play, B?" Jack asked.

Benny inclined his head, then shook it. "I'll keep Michelle company. Those dolls are calling my name."

Jack smiled. He jogged over to his bike and pedaled down the familiar road. Cars were parked in one field, which was slowly filling up. In another pasture, small children on hayrides laughed and pointed at the gathered cows and horses. A small petting zoo kept the waiting youngsters occupied, and a homemade ice cream stand was selling scoops to all comers.

The picnic was being prepped all around, and the sizzle of burgers on grills wafted over to Jack as he leaned his bike along the fence and ducked between the barbed wire. Vicky McClure, an old classmate, rode up on a beautiful golden horse with a black muzzle, mane, tail, and legs. "Hey, Jack!"

"Hey, Vicky," he replied. "Wow, what a horse! What's his name?"

"This is Captain Kirk. He's a sweet boy," she said, patting him gently, "a Spanish mustang."

Jack reached out a hand and stroked the horse's flank. "*Hola, el capitán.*" Jack rubbed his head. "He looks strong."

"He is," Vicky replied, as Captain Kirk nuzzled Jack. "And he seems to like you."

"Hey there, buddy," Jack said, gently rubbing between his eyes down to his noseband. "How's things in your galaxy?"

"You're welcome to ride him," Vicky said, beginning to dismount.

"Oh, I'd love to," Jack replied, nodding to the players gathering with their gloves and bats. "About to play some baseball. Maybe later?"

"Sure, Jack." She settled back into the saddle.

"How's our guy Macky doing?" Macky was a calf that Jack and Michelle had helped deliver in this very field.

"He's in that pen near the old barn. Ornery as all get-out."

"Protective of his, uh, friends?"

"You could say that," Vicky said, laughing. "Possessive of the cows, for sure. He's kind of a, well, a bully."

Jack whistled and shook his head, feigning disappointment. "You think you know someone."

"Well, Jack, he is a bull. It's what they do."

"Oh, wow. That's where *bully* comes from. You learn something new every day."

Vicky laughed. "Just when you think you know a language."

"Exactly," Jack said, grinning. "See you later, Vicky!"

She waved and clucked her tongue, and Captain Kirk trotted off toward the stables.

There were around twenty guys out on the field, mostly high schoolers, with a few middle schoolers there by invite only.

The Baseball with a Problem

There were a few whispers as Jack jogged up. He looked around eagerly. "We doing this?"

"Let's go," Hefty shouted as he jogged up to the gathered boys, face already red and sweating.

They picked teams, and Jack was chosen first, despite his long absence. They set the boundaries, made bases from leftover gloves, and began to play. Jack was eager to play. He saw Michelle and Benny sitting in the grass nearby, nursing Cokes and talking to one another. The game progressed as the sun slowly descended.

Jack had struggled to get his bat on the ball and felt a little off. He had a few base hits and did okay in the field, but something didn't feel quite right. Jack saw that the high school baseball coach was present among the older men watching, his keen eyes tracking Jack's every move.

Jack was up to bat at the end of the game, and his hands felt sweaty. He wiped them on his jeans and stepped close to home plate. It was the bottom of the sixth—all the innings they had agreed to play—and his team was down two runs with two out. He had runners in scoring position on second and third, but he didn't just want to get a base hit and bat them in. He wanted something more dramatic. A homer, and the game was over. He glared at Hefty, who puffed and cracked his neck.

Jack glanced over at Benny and Michelle, but they were deep in conversation and weren't watching. Jack frowned, then nodded to Hefty. The portly pitcher scowled, began his windup, then sent a speeding fastball inside. Jack swung, a hard crack sounding as the ball soared high and the gathered crowd gasped. But the blasted ball veered foul, and a collective groan rose from the spectators.

The second pitch went wide for a ball. The third was another heater, and Jack fouled it off, barely catching up to it with his swing.

"Okay, Jack," Benny called. "Hit us a homer so we can go eat!"

Jack glanced over. Benny and Michelle were standing, both with anticipation on their faces. She was watching closely, her admiration clear. His heart swelled, and he turned back to Hefty. Jack frowned, and his eyes thinned to slits. He replayed every pitch so far, and his mind whirred with subconscious calculations as he breathed deep and gently teetered the bat with a firm, practiced grip. He'd been in this position many times before. This was what he was born for.

Time to shine.

Hefty smirked and began his windup. Kicking up his leg, he fired a fastball that seemed as big and slow as any Jack had ever seen. It was his perfect pitch.

Jack watched it race past and thud into the catcher's mitt.

There was silence all around.

"Ball!" Benny called. "Had to be a ball."

"No way!" Hefty yelled. "That's a strikeout. It was on the outside edge, but it was over the plate."

"No way!" Benny shouted, and several of Jack's teammates joined in the argument.

Jack, as if coming out of a daze, raised his hand. The boys fell silent. "It was across. That's strike three. Game over."

Jack had watched as the last strike came over the plate. He'd lost the game.

Chapter Six

The
Fading Sun

Jack shook hands with the guys, congratulated the other team on their victory, then crossed to meet Michelle and Benny.

"Tough luck, Jack," Benny said. "Hefty was just lucky with that pitch. My Papaw always says, 'Even a blind hog gets an acorn every now and then.'"

"I've never taken strike three before," Jack said. "Not even in Little League."

Benny nodded. "You do usually swing."

"What's the difference?" Michelle asked. "An out's an out."

"I don't mind going down fighting," Jack said, "but just standing there? No way."

A folk band—the locally famous Lively Young Oldsters—started up on a makeshift stage near the stables, and the baseball crowd began to drift that way. Michelle took Jack's hand and started off toward the small bandstand. "You can't win them all," she said.

Jack nodded and forced a smile. The fact that Michelle was holding his hand, even for a few moments, helped ease the frustration. His heart grew lighter, and he looked around. The sun was setting over the warm green hills, and his community, the people of this place he loved so much, were gathered to celebrate their home and heritage. "I love it here," he said, a feeling of gratitude welling within, driving out the threatening edge of despair.

"Me too," Michelle agreed. "No matter what other homes I may find in my life, this will always be a home for me."

"Loving the Wayland," Jack went on, "has only made me love Myrtle more. I thought it would be the opposite."

Benny squinted into the distance and spoke with a husky catch in his throat. "What do you think is the average age of the Lively Young Oldsters?"

Jack shook his head, and Michelle laugh-snorted. Jack scowled at Benny in mock severity. "Your timing is, as usual, pretty much—"

"Perfect?" Benny interrupted.

"Yeah," Jack agreed.

"That reminds me," Benny said. "Knock knock."

Michelle smiled and answered. "Who's there?"

"Interrupting doctor."

Michelle glanced at Jack, then back at Benny. "Interrupting doctor wh—"

"You have a broken leg." Benny said flatly.

Michelle exchanged another look with Jack; then they both burst into laughter, and Benny joined in.

After the friends recovered from the knock-knock joke, Benny looked around. "You guys hungry?"

Jack rolled his eyes. "Weren't you eating during the game?"

"It was a snack, Jack," Benny snapped, "so cut me some slack."

"It was a burger and a hot dog," Michelle said. "But who cares, I could eat. I was politely waiting for Jack."

"I was too," Benny insisted. "That was all pregame. Like a mid-game pregame."

They headed toward the crowd and the sounds of the Lively Young Oldsters playing their local AM radio hit, "Lively Old Youngsters." Benny excused himself to hit the restroom while Jack paid for his and Michelle's burgers. They started eating as they made their way closer to the small bandstand.

During a hooky harmony on a thumping chorus, a higher-pitched, discordant voice sounded. Smiling faces turned sour, and the band winced and glanced around. The singing stopped; then the music stuttered and stalled.

A screaming, raging voice could be heard hollering from near the front. Jack didn't have a good angle, but he stepped sideways and saw the crowd clearing away, making an uneasy circle around one person.

"Doom is at your door, little Myrtle, and you laugh and clap and sing. Hypocrites! Fools!" Allegra shrieked. She was dressed in black, her once wild hair now a bald pate covered in green and blue tattoos. Silver piercings dotted her ears, which ended in a thick stud in each lobe. She wasn't dirty, but her face was thin and, Jack thought, alarmingly skull-like. The crowd stepped further back, and Allegra raised her hand. "Where is she? Where is Michelle Robinson?"

Much closer, another series of shrieks sounded, and their section of the crowd stepped back to reveal two young women, all dressed in black with leather and chains and strange bright dye in their spiked and oddly chopped hair. They pointed at Michelle and shrieked on and on, their eyes wide and frightening. "Here, Mother!" one called, her teeth bared in a snarl.

Jack stepped in front of Michelle as Allegra strode over and positioned herself in front of the two women, who were then joined by three more from other parts of the crowd. Allegra made a sign with her hand that the rest imitated. "So you are her guardian!" Allegra cried. "The boy hero of the twelve realms. A Waylander wonder. You think he is at some boarding school? Ha! No, he is training for war in a city between worlds. He consorts with elves and conquers monsters."

The people nearest Jack glanced at him, then back at Allegra, confused and distraught. Jack stepped closer and reached a hand back to touch Michelle's elbow. "Allegra, what are you doing? You need help."

Allegra hissed. "We need no man to command us. I am the coven mother of the Order of the Fading Sun. My sisters and I want to speak with the secret goddess you and your hypocrite sage are hiding in Myrtle. Come out, come out, Princess Michelle," she sang. "Stand behind no man. Come, young blood. My sisters and I only want a bite of your time." She laughed, and her twisted disciples showed sickly grins. "Come with us, Princess, and we'll lead you to your true home. We know where you're from and where you belong and what powers are there in that sacred city. I can make a way without a key."

Jack shook his head slowly. "It's time for you to leave, Allegra."

Allegra signaled to her sisters, and they stepped forward. That's when more figures joined Jack. He glanced left and saw his and Benny's moms, then to his right and saw Mrs. Robinson, who was holding a baseball bat.

Mrs. Robinson spoke calmly but with authority. "Young lady, you'd better get your skinny backside out of here in a hurry and take your Halloween pals with you."

"Allegra, honey, you need help," Benny's mom said gently.

Allegra grinned, her eyes fixed on Mrs. Marino. "I think it's you who needs help. You decline, old lady. I know it. See to your second son, or his fate will be worse than the first."

Benny appeared beside his mom, his face tormented with worry. "Allegra, what do you mean? Do you know what happened to Fred?"

"I am a gatebreaker in the making," Allegra replied coldly, "and I know the way to many graves."

Others were gathering close, so that the side opposite Allegra and her allies swelled. Father Lorenzo, the priest at Saint Andrew's, stood alongside Jack's pastor at Ebenezer Baptist, Reverend Long. Other men came to flank the moms.

"Go," Mrs. Robinson said. "Leave, now."

Allegra smiled her sickly smile again, then shouted loud. "Michelle Robinson, you golden goddess fallen from your high place. Come and join us and grow more knowing than you ever thought possible, and more powerful too. The invitation stands. But be warned, if you do not heed the call of the Fading Sun, ash will fly and tree will wither, city fall and children shiver."

Allegra turned away, and her band followed her into the darkness. The crowd was silent for a few moments, then gathered around Jack and Michelle and their friends. Questions came, and the adults tried to shield the kids. It was difficult, because none of the grownups were accustomed to lying. They tried to focus on the troubles Allegra had experienced and caused and how they could possibly help her. They blamed the use of drugs, which wasn't unlikely—but Allegra didn't seem sickly or insane. She seemed kind of powerful. Jack listened to the concerned questions from the community and tried to keep people away from Michelle.

"Allegra can't be helped if she don't want to be helped," Reverend Long's wife, Gloria, said, answering a nosy neighbor.

"That's true," another man said, "but the truth is that Jack and Michelle left school, and nobody knows nothing about this boarding school in North Carolina they're supposed to be at."

"Jack, you at a boarding school?" another man asked.

Father Lorenzo tried to keep the crowd back. "Give the kids some space, please. They've been through a lot."

"What do you mean, a lot?" the man asked. "Like, being in another world kind of a lot?"

Another woman nearby laughed. "Ha! Yeah, I bet ol' Jack and Michelle have been hanging 'round with elves and pixies and giants. They probably found some gold at the end of the rainbow too! Ha!"

Just then, sirens wailed, and Jack looked out over the crowd toward the road. A police car was speeding their way, trailing a cloud of dust. The crowd quieted, and everyone turned to see the squad car turn through the open gates into the field and skid to a stop fifteen feet away.

Police Chief Steve Robinson leapt from the driver's seat.

"Daddy?" Michelle said, stepping toward him.

The passenger side door popped open, and a tall man with silver hair and elven ears emerged, a sword at his side.

Chapter Seven

Ruben
of Thandalia

M aster Timman?" Jack was shocked to see him there in Myrtle.

The Thandalian pulled his hair over his ears and motioned Jack over. "We need to talk."

Ten minutes later there was a meeting inside the closed dining hall of Appalachianos: Benny and Michelle, along with their parents; Jack and his mom; and Master Timman and his daughter, So-addan, and his nephew, Tytrus.

"It's so strange to see you here," Michelle said to the three Thandalians.

Timman nodded. "And unusual for us to see you here, in your adopted home."

"This *is* her home." Mrs. Robinson's eyes held worry.

Timman bowed. "I meant no offense, Princess Mother."

"Princess Mother?" Mrs. Robinson grimaced. "Listen, I'm Amber Robinson, an ordinary mom and a cop's wife."

Chief Robinson stood up. "Okay, Sweetheart. We all love Michelle, and we are all trying to understand the challenges and opportunities Michelle's birth heritage involve. And we've got more of it to do tonight. Something's happened in Thandalia."

Michelle stood up, her face in anguish. "What is it? Oh, it's not another massacre, is it? Oh, no. Please, no."

"No, Baby," Chief Robinson said, putting his arm around his daughter. "It's not bad news at all." Steve Robinson's face still showed concern. "Timman," he said, nodding toward the Thandalian. Both he, his daughter, and his nephew were smiling.

"Thank you, Honorable Chief Steve," Timman said. "Princess Majestic, our forces have won a great victory in Thandalia."

Jack's heart swelled. "Really?"

Tytrus, adjusting his eye-patch, continued. "There was a battle on the edge of the Destronn Plain, and the Vandals were driven back to Destrow itself."

So-addan wiped at her eyes and grinned. "A victory!"

Michelle put her hands to her open mouth. "They drove them back so far?"

"Farther, my lady," Timman said. "Our forces retook Destrow and drove the enemy off the plain altogether."

Michelle smiled, tears shining in her eyes. Steve put his arm around her. "It's too wonderful, Daddy."

"It *is* wonderful," came a familiar voice from near the door. Jack and everyone else turned to see Joseph Wheeler, in full sage's dress, with the Prism Blade by his side. "It is a victory the like of which we have not seen for years, thanks be to God."

Wheeler crossed to join the group, and Jack noticed that some of the parents were still confused. "Joe," Uncle Freddie said, a little startled by the news and by seeing him dressed like this, "can you break this down for us a little? I'm lost."

"Certainly, Alfredo," Wheeler said, sitting down and accepting a plastic cup of pop from Benny. "Thank you. Did you mix the grape and orange?"

Benny nodded and shot him a thumbs-up. "Of course. Grorange pop. Always."

"Thank you, Benito." Turning to Benny's dad, he took a sip and continued. "As you all know, there is war in Thandalia, with the native side fighting for their homeland against Rancast's wicked allies led by Becker Ghistalli. Ghistalli is a cruel warlord and disciple of Rancast's teachings. They have controlled much of the world, including two critical cities. One of them is Destrow on the famous plain. But they overreached in a recent battle and, after a surprising loss, lost more and more ground to an aggressive counterattack led by a Thandalian Ranger captain called Bon-hadden."

"Uncle Freddie," Jack said, "Bon-hadden is like a General Patton type. Not *the* main guy, but definitely *a* main guy."

Timman nodded. "He is a brave hero and among Thandalia's finest."

Wheeler continued. "The counterattack proved so effective that the Thandalians kept going and ended an astonishing rout that resulted in the recapture of Destrow. Forces poured in over the following hours, and, I am astonished to say it, but the city is held by Captain Bon-hadden—by the Thandalian army. In fact, the enemy has been driven back to the cliffs, and the surrounding towns are liberated as well."

Michelle clenched her fists and fairly shook with joy. "This is an answer to prayer," she said. "I have dreamed of this kind of victory for so long." Then her face turned serious. "But the soldiers, they'll need medical supplies. Food. More support. I have to go to the Low Sanctum. We must support our soldiers. There will be so many needs!"

"There is a need," Wheeler said, crossing to kneel in front of her. "You have done more for the care of the Thandalian soldiers than anyone, to be sure. You have worked tirelessly to aid them and their families. But the sages' council believes you can do more."

Michelle nodded, resolute. "Anything." Behind her, Mrs. Robinson's face twisted in deep concern.

Timman stood again, pacing. "Sage Wheeler, you know I respect you like no other, and I should never wish to contradict you, but—"

"I know, Consul Timman," Wheeler said, raising his hands. "I share your concerns. And I appreciate why you wanted to go straight to Steve when you heard news of our proposal. But nevertheless, the proposal must be made."

"What is it?" Michelle asked eagerly.

Wheeler clasped his hands together. "The sages' council believes it is time for you to appear in Thandalia. The council, with surprising unanimity, believes that if you come to liberated Destrow and inspire the Thandalian forces—perhaps the way you did on the festival's eighth day—then the war might be won in a week."

"The advantage is there," Tytrus said, rising to his feet with enthusiasm. "The Thandalian Rangers agree with the council. The war could be over. It could push us over the edge."

"The war could be over," So-addan said. "Think of it!"

Jack felt divided by deep concern for Michelle's protection and the thrilling possibility of victory in Thandalia.

Master Timman looked from his nephew to Michelle.

"My dear Thaon Majestic and prized student." Timman was Michelle and Jack's tutor in Thandalian studies. He was the one who had told them both all that was known about Andos, that golden city of the Thaons and the place of Michelle's birth. His face was pinched in worry. "I know you have longed to see Thandalia, and especially Andos itself, that holy city. I have told you of your sacred place on that mountain. But I urge caution here. I know this might push the war to an end, but I am not sure it is worth the risk. If we keep our most prized asset back—pardon the phrase—we have options. As I told Sage Wheeler, with all respect, Chief Steve, I think it's too early to bring the Princess Majestic into the conflict like this."

Mrs. Robinson nodded. "First sensible thing I've heard all night. Listen, high lords and sages, this is my little girl. She's still a child. Right, Steve?" She looked to her husband.

Chief Steve Robinson had his head down, face in his hands. He looked up, and tears stood out in his eyes. "Some of you don't know this," here he looked at Sarah, then to Jack, "but I've been to Thandalia. I went there with Ruben Zulu, but I didn't return with him. I buried my best friend on a hillside outside Andos and came home with a beautiful baby girl."

Jack hugged his mother. She looked over at Steve, blinking tears. "Why . . . . Steve . . . why, why didn't you tell us?"

Steve wiped at his eyes. "I'm sorry, Sarah. Jack, forgive me. I'm so sorry. It has pained me for fourteen years, but I gave my word I would tell no one else."

"Gave your word to who?" Jack asked, anger rising inside him.

Steve rubbed at his mouth, creases forming around his pinched eyes. "I gave my word to the sage who gave me my daughter: Joseph Wheeler." Jack looked over at Wheeler with astonished eyes. Wheeler nodded somberly. Chief Robinson went on. "He relieved me of that burden recently, and I know he has good reasons for that. I've been trying to figure out how to tell you everything—because I feel so sorry about having kept this from you for so long. Ruben died protecting Michelle while the Thaons were slaughtered by that murderer Rancast. I saw them killed. I saw Ruben . . . fall . . . I saw it all."

Benny gasped. "You saw Rancast?"

Wiping his face with his hands, Steve Robinson looked up. "Rancast killed Ruben. I got away with my girl. It was the worst and best day of my life." He looked at Jack and his mother. "I am so sorry to you both. I am so sorry I couldn't bring Ruben home too."

Jack's heart hurt, and he squeezed his mom tighter as tears rolled down his face.

Wheeler spoke into the silence. "Steve and Ruben were caught up in a battle in which they did not enlist, but they both fought bravely when the moment came. Steve did what I asked and left with the baby. Ruben died protecting their retreat. Rancast desecrated the sacred city of Andos and slaughtered the Thaons. He took the fruit and procured his greatest enhancement—becoming far more powerful than he was good enough to become. It was a dark day for your family, Sarah and Jack, a dark day for Thandalia, and a dark day for all the worlds."

"Did he say the Twenty-Third Psalm?" Mom asked.

Wheeler and Chief Robinson nodded.

"He died well, then," Mom said, and she rose and slowly crossed to Chief Robinson. "Come now, Steve. All is forgiven, my brother. All is forgiven." They embraced, and Mrs. Robinson joined in, tears flowing freely. Michelle reached for Jack's hand, and he let her take it, and they joined the hug as well.

In the quiet, Michelle turned to Wheeler and nodded. "I'm going," she whispered. "I am going."

Jack paid attention as the adults talked on and on, with asides taken in private by each family, followed by more discussions by the whole group. But he was distracted. He thought of his beloved father, fallen in the cause of fighting Rancast and rescuing Michelle. His admiration grew for his father, while his sorrow at such a terrible loss surged up again. Anger at Rancast, already present, flared on the edge of rage. Jack felt anger swell inside and pass through him, first at Steve, and then at Wheeler for keeping this secret from him. But Jack knew it wasn't Wheeler's fault. Rancast killed his father. In Jack's pocket he carried Ruben Zulu's police chief badge, and his hand kept going to it again and again.

They were hours talking in Appalachianos, but Michelle and her father, and eventually her mother too, all agreed that she should go to Thandalia, to the Destronn Plains and Destrow itself.

"But I'll go along," Chief Robinson said, "and I get to be in on every decision about her protection. And I'm never far from her."

"Of course," Wheeler agreed. "You are her father."

"I'm coming too," Jack said. His mother squeezed his hand but did not object.

"I shall lead the excursion," Wheeler said, patting Mrs. Robinson's hand. "If at any time I believe she is in direct danger, I will get her out of there, so I will."

Tytrus knelt before Michelle. "This truly could end the war," he said, his eye full of light. "You could end the war, Princess, just as you drove out the crow horde on that festival day."

So-addan knelt beside her cousin. "For the first time in ages, we have the two good words."

"Light," Jack whispered.

"And hope," Benny added.

Michelle nodded solemnly. Then she smiled.

Benny was allowed to go, but Uncle Freddie was reluctantly convinced that he could stay home and care for their business amidst the troubles they faced—without any dishonor. He was willing and eager to go along but was persuaded by Wheeler that a small group, including some key Thandalian rangers who were best equipped for this mission, would be sufficient. Tytrus and Jack would go as protectors. So-addan would go along as Michelle's attendant—required by custom. Michelle happily approved of that choice.

The party broke up, and Jack walked outside with his mother as fireworks rose into the night sky over Myrtle.

Wheeler stepped into the center of the families. "Be with the ones you love tonight, and we shall meet at the gate at dawn. Timman, Tytrus, and So-addan, shall I escort you back into the Wayland?" The three Thandalians bade everyone goodnight and followed Wheeler up Sequoyah Street, toward the park.

The families prayed then and went their separate ways.

Jack's mom hugged the other mothers in turn, and it was a long time before Mrs. Robinson released her. Finally, tears in her eyes again, she crossed back to Jack. "It's a beautiful night," she said. "Let's walk home."

Jack nodded, and they set off, walking slowly. "Are you worried?"

Mom looked over at him as they began walking. "Of course. I can't help it. You must come back to me, Jack, if you can."

"I will. I prom—" he began, but Mom interrupted.

"Don't make any promises, son. Let your yes be yes, and only when you can be sure. I know you. The cavalier poet said, 'I could not love thee dear, so much, loved I not honor more.' You are like that man—like your father. I know you will try, son, to come back to me. But I release you to do what's right. I give you to God."

Jack put his arm around her as they turned up Sequoyah Street. "If Michelle really can help end the war, then we have to try. And this might be the best way to keep me safe. If the war is over, that's good news for all mothers and sons."

"Always know that you are loved," she said. "Be what you're called to be. I think that Rancast believes he needs to be more than a man. But he's wrong. A man's what God made you to be, son. So be that, and while you're at it, you might as well go ahead and be the best one you can be."

Chapter Eight

Thandalia, Ho!

L ong before sunrise Jack was awake and working. Mom helped him, and together they filled his backpack with everything they thought he might need. His Walkman, which he knew he'd have to leave behind, blasted "Are You Ready for the Country" by Neil Young while he packed. Jack dressed in his acolyte uniform, as requested. All except for the boots, which he stuffed into his bag, opting for his Jordans instead.

Jack's bike was still in town, so Mom drove him to the park. They said their goodbyes, and Jack walked into the dark forest. Crossing into the Ancient Glade, in a few minutes he reached the clearing in front of the gate tree, lit by a few lanterns. He saw that Wheeler and Steve were already there, along with Benny and Michelle. Michelle looked beautiful in her Thandalian tunic. Wheeler wore the Prism blade, and Benny—sporting his Appalachianos T-shirt and jean jacket— was armed with his sword, too.

"Thanks for dressing up, B," Jack said.

Benny shrugged. "In many cultures, a shirt that both looks

and," he bent to sniff the shirt, "yes—smells—like pizza is considered very valuable and classy."

Jack shook his head. "I'm sure the Thandalians will be in awe."

"Fear not. I packed a variety of pizza-smelling tees for their viewing and olfactory—yeah, I just said that—pleasure."

Steve inhaled deeply and rubbed his chin. He wore jeans, a wide-brimmed hat, and a light button-up shirt. His service revolver hung at his side. Each was standing by a horse, and Wheeler held out the reins to a beautiful golden mount with black around its muzzle, mane, and legs.

"Captain Kirk?" Jack asked. "Is that you, boy?"

"Aye," Wheeler said, releasing the reins. He also handed Jack two large green pills. "For the journey. The sun there is of a different intensity, and this will help your body adjust, so it will."

Benny's face convulsed. "It tastes great, Jack. You'll love it."

Great. Jack grabbed his canteen and threw back the pills. They tasted like old rust and vomit, but he choked them down and swigged some water. "Oof. That's got to be worse than whatever it's helping."

"That's what I said," Benny agreed. "I think Wheeler's just testing our mettle by making us taste . . . well, corroded metal. He wants us to feel grateful when we eat exploding ants for dinner tonight."

"You know what we are eating, Benito," Wheeler said, "because you shall be preparing it."

Benny glanced at Michelle and Jack. "Hope you guys like exploding ants."

"Come along," Wheeler said. "We must get through the

Thandalian gate before the suns rise in the Wayland."

Wheeler turned to the gate and extended the key, "*Clavis Ignum*," and they led their horses through. It was dark on the Wayland side as well. The plan was to draw as little attention as possible to this mission. The enemy spy network was active, even there in the Wayland. Sage Raftereen, who was well-known as a sympathizer to Rancast, had a compound where Wheeler believed he sheltered many dangerous persons and encouraged their plots. Jack kept his eyes peeled, half-expecting to see the bald gray-skinned sage in his flowing robe peeking from behind a corner. *No. He'll have his agents out. And they could be of any race.*

They mounted and rode along the foggy wall by the river. Jack, who had ridden horses a few times, urged Captain Kirk up beside Michelle. "Good morning, m'lady."

"Morning, Jack." Michelle was riding a beautiful black horse and was dressed in a white tunic with golden trim and leggings beneath. She wore her hair up in a regal style with jewels throughout.

"Are you comfortable?" he asked.

She shrugged. "More comfortable than it looks."

Jack smiled. "In case you're wondering, I'm comfortable too."

They heard a splash behind them, and Jack turned his horse back to see Benny, barely mounted as he slipped down the side of his saddle, and his horse up to its belly in the river.

Chief Robinson nodded to Wheeler. "We'll catch up." He turned his horse back and was soon by Benny's side, hoisting him back up and leading them back to the shore. Wheeler moved ahead.

Steve Robinson frowned at Benny. "First time?"

Benny exhaled slowly. "During the whole 'who is going on this mission' convo, I may have possibly overestimated my horsing-around experience just a tad."

"I think you estimated about right," Steve muttered as he and Benny rejoined the rest of the party.

Jack shook his head as he and Michelle followed Wheeler.

Jack was smiling, and he glanced over at Michelle. She wasn't. "Are you okay?"

"Big day for me, Jack," she replied. "I've been dreaming of this for a long time."

Jack smiled. "About a year and a half, I guess." That was around the time when she had learned about the Wayland and, soon after, that she was a Thaon from Thandalia.

"No," she said quietly. "It's been much longer."

They rode on in silence till they passed the broken gate of Kaalgrad. The stone wall surrounding the apparently dead tree was riddled with spidering cracks. Ash-gray limbs seemed brittle enough to break off, and the ground surrounding the tree was brown and burned.

This was where Rancast had escaped. This was where Jack had killed the monster Mordok. This was where Michelle had grown golden wings and flown over the astounded Thandalians. Fire from her brightness destroyed a horde of enemy crows, large beastly birds with teeth and terrible claws that had preyed on the frightened refugees. She had been their savior that day, their light and hope. Looking at her now, she had the look of what she was. Michelle Robinson was more than the girl he'd had a crush on for years. She was more than the talented kid from school. She was more than simply gifted and beautiful. How much more?

Jack's breath caught as they continued past the Kaalgrad gate. Here they had fought countless huge crows and would have fallen had it not been for Michelle's amazing transformation. Kaalgrad's gate was a dead door to a dying world, so they pushed ahead toward the gate tree leading to Thandalia. Thandalia was alive but immersed in a terrible war that had gone on for years. Jack wasn't afraid of the fight or of the danger to himself. He tried to think rationally about what he was afraid of. It wasn't exactly for Michelle's safety. He was concerned about that, of course, but it wasn't what dug at him. He decided he was afraid that, on this trip, Michelle would become so much more of who she could become that he would be left far behind.

A thought hit him like an arrow from the shadows. A thought so clear it seemed to be spoken in his mind. He glanced back at the Kaalgrad gate, then, grimacing, ahead at Michelle, whose horse was drifting further ahead of him. The thought was stuck in his mind, and it felt indisputably true.

To be with her, I have to be the greatest.

"We're gonna get left behind," Chief Robinson said, riding up behind with one hand holding Benny's reins. "We've got to keep up, boys."

Jack nodded. "Yes, sir. I do. I mean, we do."

Benny grinned apologetically at Jack. "Don't want to bring shame on the Myrtle contingent, do we? I mean, more shame. Don't want to bring even more shame than I have already broughten upon us. My bad, guys. I'll get the hang of it." He lay low on the saddle, hugging his horse's neck. But he seemed to be slipping sideways again. "I saw *High Noon*, so I've done a little bit of research. Plus, I'm a quick learner if you give me plenty of time. I'm on the edge, fellas—the edge of mastery."

Chief Robinson sighed. "You're on the edge of falling off again." Jack, with a glance at Michelle as she rode alongside Wheeler and drew still further ahead, circled back to push Benny back up in the saddle. Chief Robinson handed Benny the horse's reins again. Benny gripped them in a fist that was already clenched in the poor creature's mane.

"What's your horse's name?" Jack asked. It was a lovely appaloosa with a cookies and cream mix of white and black speckled across its legs, belly, and face.

"Ozzie," Benny replied. "I think after Ozzie and Harriet, that old show."

"Are they all TV names?" Jack asked. "I didn't know the McClures owned a TV."

"Mine's Harriet," Chief Robinson said flatly.

"I guess," Benny replied, smiling up at the stolid chief, "that me and you are gonna be best—"

"Don't say it," Chief Robinson said.

"Sorry, Chief." Benny saluted. "I just hope we can be pals. I am a big police supporter."

Chief Robinson pursed his lips. "You mean you've seen a bunch of cop movies?"

Benny squinted, then nodded. "That probably sums it up."

"Thought so. And you boys better just call me Steve." He peered ahead to try to see Michelle and Wheeler, then looked back at the boys. "I'm off duty on this mission. I'm off police business," he continued, with a hard look at Jack, "and on to taking care of my daughter business. This is the only job in any world that I care about right now. And I will do whatever it takes to protect her."

"Understood, sir," Jack said. "I feel the same way."

"Sometimes what boys feel changes," Steve said, "but what a father must do for his little girl never changes, no matter what happens or who comes along." He kicked his horse and trotted forward, leaving Jack and Benny to exchange a look, eyebrows raised.

Benny whistled. "Looks like he's worried about more than just Rancast's guys. He's got his eye on you, Jack."

"I kind of thought we'd maybe be bonding over his experience with my dad on his last trip to Thandalia," Jack replied. "I thought it would be on his mind."

Benny nodded, raising up a moment from his neck-hugging riding position, then quickly resuming it at the first sign of slipping. "He probably is thinking about it, Jack. That's probably why he's feeling a little concerned."

Jack shrugged and took a last look at the huge Wayland flag—with its tree-and-roots emblem—flying from the topmost tower of the Gock. "Be right back," he said. "Stay well."

Benny nodded. "So long, tower; so long, tree; so long, delicious things to eat."

Jack urged Benny's horse ahead with a click. Ozzie nodded and trotted up beside Jack and Captain Kirk. "Okay, boys," Jack said, patting his horse and looking ahead as the predawn light showed their fellow travelers ahead passing through the gate into Thandalia. "It's time to explore a strange new world."

Chapter Nine

In and
Out of Gate City

J ack came last, following Benny, who was still draped over Ozzie, hugging the horse's neck. The dawn was not far off in the Wayland, but an astonishingly bright light met Jack's gaze as he rode, ducking as he passed through the tree gate and entered Thandalia. It took a little while for his eyes to adjust to the glare as his horse whinnied and stepped sideways, then regained his stride and followed the others in a line. Jack blinked and wiped at his eyes, trying to focus.

As his eyes adjusted, he saw golden sand beneath a purple sky that held a white sun, small and distant. A rising landscape of rock covered with gray brush and tough wiry trees surrounded them. They were in a canyon, with a bombed-out town surrounding the gate tree. He saw a roadway, orange soil and rock exposed, leading up and out of the canyon. A strange series of boarded-up buildings leaned against a hillside covered in scrub with slick luminescent rocks revealed beneath its surface, showing a strange array of warped colors. The rocks seemed like bubble solution, with purples and blues swirling around an eerie transparency. The devastated town was full of refugee tents, huts, and hovels that stretched in every direction. A garrison fort loomed on the edge of town, with soldiers patrolling the perimeter. There was a kind of temple, or church-like building, that was similar to the House of Thandal in the Wayland. The beautiful sanctuary featured bent old men stooped on the steps. This tiny slice of Thandalia came to him in splashes of gold and white, orange and purple. He thought of ancient Greece or Israel and the American frontier west of a century before, his mind trying to make sense of the strange surroundings. The town and its sprawling refugee camp was some distance away, but Jack saw children playing in the lanes, and his heart sank to think of what they had been through. He rode over beside Michelle.

Michelle looked over at him, her eyes shining while her face kept a composed look. She inhaled deeply, eyes closing a moment as she filled her lungs with the air of her native land. Opening her eyes again, she dismounted in an elegant, effortless kick and slide, landing to gaze at the distant peaks and all around the war-torn town. The Thandalian contingent knelt at her approach, then rose and stood reverently. They held the reins of several six-legged horses common in the Wayland, a few of the largest ones heaped high with supplies and clearly not meant for riding. Consul Timman and his daughter, So-addan, stood alongside one-eyed Tytrus and three Thandalian rangers. Jack didn't know two of them, though he had seen them before. The one he knew was Dohlun, a classmate of Tytrus's and a former opponent of Jack's in Pavilion Siege.

"Majesty Bright," Timman said, hands clasped together, "light and hope to you this glorious day—a day we have all been waiting for. It is not what it once was, nor what we hope it will be again, but welcome to Gate City, and to Thandalia, your home."

Michelle turned to him and almost dipped her head to bow, but, recollecting herself, she raised her head high. Jack knew this was out of respect for them. "Light and hope, my countryman. Thank you for accompanying us on our mission. I see," she said, glancing around, "that our company makes up a lucky eleven. A good omen."

Timman smiled at So-addan, and Tytrus at the rangers. Their expressions said, *See, she knows our ways.* So-addan stepped forward and bowed low, and Jack saw that Timman's face was radiant with pride. She crossed to Michelle's side. "Eleven *is* lucky, Princess. I am So-addan, daughter of Timman, and I am—in life or death or between the worlds—your servant."

Michelle nodded. "Beloved daughter of Timman, you are my servant, and I take you in my charge under this sun and above these sands. Some water, now."

So-addan bowed and hurried to one of the packed animals to fetch a canteen of water.

Michelle whispered to Jack. "It's considered rude if a first command isn't issued immediately upon agreeing to service. Feels weird to us, but I want to honor their customs—I mean, our customs."

Jack nodded and whispered back, "You're doing great."

So-addan handed the canteen to Michelle. Michelle took a short drink, then offered some back. So-addan glanced at her father, who nodded and smiled, and she drank too. She grinned at Michelle, and the Thandalians seemed happy.

"Seeing a lot of passing around the old H-2-O," Benny said, still hugging Ozzie around the neck, "but what's the snack situation like? Anyone else starving, and do we have to feed Michelle every time before we can eat?"

Jack shook his head. "Benny, what is wrong with you?"

Benny shrugged. "Hunger pangs?"

"I tell you what," Steve said, "whenever you learn to sit up on your horse like a man, then maybe you can eat something. I brought sardines."

Benny's nose wrinkled, and he eased up in the saddle, finally sitting upright, his smile tight and his eyes fearful. "Am I doing it, Steve?"

"Sort of. Just relax, kid. It's an animal. It can sense your fear."

Benny breathed out in a jagged, nervous exhalation. "Ozzie there, easy . . . I mean, easy there, Ozzie. I'm not going to eat you."

"Eat you?" Steve winced over at Benny. "Boy, who's talking about eating this horse? Just calm down."

Benny saluted, his hand darting back to grab the reins again. "Yes, Commander, er, Captain . . . er Captain Chief Steve. There was talk of snacks and eating a few moments ago, and I didn't want Ozzie to get the wrong idea. We've all heard people say it. I've said it a million times." He went on, whispering. "I'm so hungry I could eat a—" He broke off and pointed down at Ozzie.

Jack rolled his eyes and dismounted. While Michelle spoke apart with Steve and Wheeler, he handed his reins to Benny and crossed to Tytrus. They engaged in their familiar handshake, then walked over to the pack horses as Tytrus secured another bag onto one of the hulking creatures. "It's a good day to try," Tytrus said.

Jack nodded, finishing their saying. "And that's a good day to die."

"The stakes were a little lower in those games of Pavilion Siege," Tytrus said, scanning Gate City. It was an arresting settlement, lovely in many ways, but scarred all over.

Jack rubbed his chin. "They always felt high in Pav."

"For me too. But you always knew, Jack, who the real fight was with. It will be such a blow to Rancast if she can pull this off."

"Your world is beautiful, Ty."

"It was," he replied. "It will be again."

A dirty refugee boy, elf-eared and bright-eyed, appeared from behind one of the pack horses.

"Hey, little guy," Jack said. "What are you doing over here?"

"*Lifton humm-un do-allska non,*" the boy replied.

Tytrus laughed. "He doesn't want us to tell on him and he's asking what's wrong with your ears."

Jack smiled. "Tell him I lost the tips in a bad haircut."

Tytrus knelt and spoke to the boy in his own language. The conversation went back and forth, Tytrus nodding as the child explained his situation, pointing to the rim of the canyon, then over to the camp. Tytrus winced, then looked up at Jack. "His name is Rowl-dun. His friends call him Dunny. He's been here for six weeks. He's from Freston village, not too far from Gate City Canyon. He says Freston was firebombed by . . ." he turned to Dunny and asked, "*Du-ann cole hunta frah?*"

Dunny looked down. "*Ginta cole hah frah-zola. Horvuh callum don, qua-Thao-rum sune rello-foar.*"

Tytrus put his hand on the boy's shoulder. "He says they came in the night and seemed to attack from the sky. Like the

Thaons of old days, but against us. Thaons against us."

Jack glanced over at Michelle, then back at Dunny. "I'm sorry," he said, kneeling in front of the boy. Then, remembering his basic Thandalian, he added, "*Rotar-hanum, Dunny.*"

Dunny stepped forward and reached for Jack's ears. He felt the rounded tops and grimaced, suppressing a shudder. Then he laughed. Jack joined the laughter and patted his head. "I hope we have good news for you soon, little guy."

Tytrus spoke to him a moment longer, pointing. Dunny nodded and, with one last glance back at Jack, ran back toward the camp. There, on the edge of the sad settlement, a crowd was gathering. A weary mother bent and gathered Dunny in her arms, holding him tightly as they all looked on at the strange company near the fabled gate tree.

"Do they know about Michelle?" Jack asked.

"They hear rumors and reports," Tytrus replied, "but when you've seen what they've seen, you're reluctant to believe anything that stirs your hope."

"Some of them seem to still believe." Jack saw several who knelt reverently on the ground, including Dunny's mother. She whispered in his ear, and he knelt as well, assuming a reverent posture and side-eying his mother for approval.

Wheeler called for attention. Jack and Tytrus hurried back to the group, and everyone turned to Wheeler. The old sage looked around, then over at the distant sun. "It is an hour till noon, and we must complete our first leg of this journey at once."

Timman frowned. "Sage Wheeler, I thought we agreed to trek the first leg after some time for the princess to adjust in our world—here in Gate City."

Wheeler shook his head. "We agreed, above all, that I would lead us. Now, everyone mount up. At once, do you hear me?" he snapped. He drew a small horn from his vest and blew a long note. Jack eyed Michelle as she leapt back into her saddle.

Steve eased his horse, Harriet, closer to them both. "Stay sharp, Zulu. Your only job is to make sure Benny keeps up. I'm with Michelle."

Jack nodded and climbed back into the saddle on Captain Kirk. He wondered if Steve had ever uttered those words to his father. *Stay sharp, Zulu.*

They heard a noise of horses and low commands. From out of a nearby barn-like building came a large group of riders. They were dressed in familiar garb. Jack realized they looked familiar because they were dressed to look like them, the party of eleven. Jack counted at least five more groups of eleven, each with a girl who looked something like Michelle riding in its center alongside a servant.

Wheeler raised his hand as the riders circled him. "You know your duty. Ride!" He turned his horse and snapped the reins. "Get on!"

Steve and Michelle followed Wheeler, making for the trees to the right of the refugee camp.

"Come on, Benny!" Jack cried.

They followed Wheeler, Steve, and Michelle, as the rest of their company weaved through the chaos of the scrum of riders all around to join in the train.

Benny's eyes bulged as he clung to Ozzie's back. Jack's eyes darted from Benny to their band ahead and over to the many groups of eleven departing in different directions all over Gate City. They were riding fast, but Benny was not okay.

"Ja-a-a-a-ck!" Benny cried as he bounced and dangled, half off the saddle.

Jack swerved a darting rider. The groups broke increasingly apart the farther from the gate tree they went, and Jack rode close to Benny. He hoisted Benny up with one hand, the other clinging to Captain Kirk's reins. Benny seemed settled for the moment, but their company was shooting ahead in a trail of rising dust, and they were being left behind. The steep climb up the canyon was just ahead after a long run to the edge of the scrub forest. Steve glanced back at the distance widening between the two boys and the group and shook his head. Jack wrinkled his nose in a grimace. *You think I'm failing my first assignment on this mission?*

"Sit back!" Jack shouted, motioning for Benny to ease back in Ozzie's saddle.

Benny, with a terrified glance around, reluctantly did as Jack said. Jack kept hold of his reins but raised his right leg and planted it on top of his own saddle. Loosening his foot in the left stirrup, he balanced, leaning left as the horses drew closer.

Benny's mouth fell open. "What?" he said stupidly, absent-mindedly jerking the reins so that Ozzie pitched left. *Too late!* Jack was already leaping. He dug in harder and released the reins he had meant to hold, driving into a diving leap. He landed half on Benny's horse, his arms burning as he dragged himself up, finally righting himself in the saddle ahead of a gaping Benny.

"Hey, B," Jack said, breathing hard. He gripped the reins on Ozzie and nudged him right, toward Captain Kirk. Riding close, he caught up his horse's reins and then kicked Ozzie into a faster gallop. "Let's go!" he shouted. "H'ya! H'ya!"

They sped ahead, closing the gap and soon falling in line behind the last in their train, racing away up the hidden forest path ascending the canyon.

Now that they had caught up, Jack had time to look around again. They weren't following the main road. Another company of eleven decoy riders went that way. He saw the dust rising from several spots in the canyon as they climbed, but each band was disappearing in the distance now. He turned back to Benny. "You okay, bro?"

"Humiliated? Yes. Otherwise, fine."

"No one saw, B. It's okay."

"Michelle saw," Benny said. "I had a good view of the whole thing, sitting there like a baby in a car seat. She saw it all, and Steve had to keep her going."

"So you're not a great horseman, yet," Jack replied. "We'll have time to get better. Ozzie's just not used to you yet."

"Hey, don't be putting down my horse. Ozzie's a good boy." He patted the horse's flank.

"He just needs to stick a little closer to Harriet," Jack said, "and to keep you in the saddle."

Benny coughed. "I could have possibly been a little more help on that front."

"Don't beat yourself up," Jack said. "Let me do it." He elbowed Benny playfully.

They rode on, rising after nearly an hour's riding onto the rim of the orange-hued canyon. From there, they headed east and a little north, through a valley between high hills, then north, away from those hills. At times, rocks seemed to grow from the ground. In strange-shaped formations, they dotted the landscape. Some seemed to be stretching grasping hands at the violet sky; others were oddly balanced rocks and craggy boulders.

They rode past several strange outcroppings till they came to a wide desert plain and seemed to aim at a colossal rock formation, high and isolated. Over the next hours, they drew closer and closer to the distant rocks, which Jack believed were orange at the top, fading to white at their roots in the golden sand. The orange sand of the Gate City Canyon gave way to more golden brown ground here, hard-packed along their path. The closer they got, the more forbidding the rock formation became. It seemed as high as a small mountain. They continued to ride hard, and Jack grew concerned for the horses, especially Ozzie, who was carrying two. As they drew nearer, Jack saw that a narrow gap formed a path between the rock formation, which was really two giant translucent rocks leaning against one another, connecting in several places but with many openings between. They rode toward the base of these orange-topped giants. As they slowed, still a few miles away, Jack brought Ozzie to a full stop. He dismounted and got Benny secure in the saddle again. He leapt onto Captain Kirk, and they quickly caught up again with the slower-moving company.

Soon they nearly reached the rocks themselves, and Wheeler called a halt in their vast shadows. "We stop here, friends. We must let the horses drink and rest. We will spend the evening here and ride on again at dawn. See to your tents. Well done, everyone."

Timman dismounted and crossed to Wheeler. "Well done, indeed, Sage Wheeler. That was well conceived and executed."

"Thank you, Consul," Wheeler replied, dismounting. "I hope it helped to throw off any of Ghistalli's Vandal spies."

Tytrus walked over. "Sage Wheeler, are we not going the wrong way for Destrow? Why not go due west here? The Destronn Plain is not this way. The Brothers," he said, motioning to the giant rocks, "mark the way to the road to the Golden City."

Michelle drew close, with Steve beside her. She looked hopeful. "Are we going, at last, to Andos itself?"

Chapter Ten

Shots
and Promises

No," Wheeler said. "We are not going to Andos. That is not possible now. Far too dangerous and . . . well, it is out of the question. Our mission is the Destronn Plain, as planned. We are simply going a roundabout way. The road beyond the Brothers," and here he motioned toward the giant rocks, "will take us there."

"To throw off the enemy," Steve said. "Joe's plan worked perfectly. We have a mission here, and we agreed we're going to stick to it. No surprises. We are definitely not going to Andos."

Michelle's brows knit, and her eyes lost a touch of their luster, but she nodded.

"You knew about this?" Jack asked Steve.

Steve didn't reply, only took a long drink from his canteen.

"Get settled in for the night," Wheeler said. "It gets cold, to be sure, so you shall need your tents and blankets. Tytrus, if you please, take another man and secure the perimeter."

"Aye, sir," Tytrus replied, nodding to Dohlun, who joined him as they grabbed rifles from their saddlebags and began their sweep on foot.

"Cool guns," Benny said to no one in particular. Steve frowned, seemed to pause and consider a moment, then began digging in his own saddlebag.

Jack and Benny led their horses to the makeshift pen the other rangers had made for the animals and saw that they were watered and fed. So-addan was waiting on Michelle, busily working to make their tent comfortable for the princess. Michelle was clearly trying to help without going against the customs of her station. She seemed a little frustrated.

The boys began setting up their tent, and Benny took the lead. He was fast and efficient and had it up in five minutes. Steve appeared, half-scowling at Jack. He looked like a cowboy, his wide hat cocked a little and his sidearm hanging low off his belt. Steve hadn't shaved in a few days. His black mustache now had the shadow of a beard around it.

Jack stepped closer to him. "You've been here before, sir?"

Steve nodded. "I have. Walk with me, Jack?"

Benny shot Jack a thumbs-up. "I'm going to get working on dinner."

Steve motioned to a bag that sat next to Benny in the pile of food supplies. "Do you have any of those pop cans left?" Benny had smuggled in a six-pack of Coke with their provisions for the journey and had somehow already consumed all six since setting up camp.

"Sure." Benny held up a small pouch that contained the six empty cans, as well as various other trash items that he had accumulated.

Steve led Jack out into the Thandalian desert, far enough that the bustling noises of camp became faint. Beyond the Brothers, he saw the distant peaks of high mountains.

They said nothing, keeping the silence for a long while as they walked. Finally, Steve stopped. "I've got something for you, Jack." He pulled out another revolver that had been tucked into the belt behind his back. "It's your dad's service revolver. I've been taking care of it for years, meaning to give it to you. Considering the threats we may face, it seems like the right time."

"Thank you." Jack received it reverently. They were quiet for a while once again, while Jack examined the weapon. "Was he using it when . . . ?"

"Yes," Steve replied. "He fired his last shot defending Michelle and me. He tried to kill Rancast, but that villain would not die. Ruben slowed him down, though, and we got away. Like I said, it was the best and worst day of my life."

"Rancast has to fall." Jack ran his hand over the gun's barrel. "Or Michelle will never be safe. No one will be. He'll come for it all."

"It's true," Steve agreed. "We either bow the knee to him or cut him down. There's no in between anymore. Not with him. I'm sure of that."

Jack nodded, checking the chambers. "Do you have his holster, sir?"

"It's back in my saddlebag. You know how to use that?"

"Kind of," Jack replied. "My mom's brother, Uncle Nathan, has taken me shooting a few times. He's a firearms instructor."

"I know Nate," Steve said. "We've used him for training on the force. He's a good guy."

"He is," Jack agreed. "We mostly shot with rifles, but we did shoot a revolver a few times. Sir, will us shooting give away our location?"

"Wheeler assures me we're okay here," Steve replied. "The smoke from our fire is a bigger problem, but we've planned for it all. Don't worry; just get ready to shoot."

Jack nodded. "Ready."

"Let's see what you got," Steve said, crossing to set up the six empty Coke cans on small luminous rocks. Returning, he said, "Remember, the most dangerous kind of weapon in the world is an unloaded gun."

Jack nodded. *He means people think it's unloaded, and that's how really bad accidents happen.* It was something Uncle Nathan had taught him.

Jack opened the cylinder and saw that the revolver was fully loaded. He snapped the cylinder closed. He set his feet, breathed as normally as possible, then carefully cocked the revolver. Jack jerked the trigger. The handgun leaped back in his grip, and the loud report came, echoing off the huge rock walls.

The cans were unharmed.

Jack frowned. "Thought I had 'em in my sights."

"Try again," Steve said.

Jack settled himself, tried to relax, and cocked the hammer back once again. Again, he fired.

Nothing. *Missed again?*

His ears rang and he frowned, frustrated that he could see no results. His embarrassment edging higher and his anger kicking in, he fired the last four rounds in succession, gritting his teeth with a growl.

The cans were untouched.

Jack kicked the ground. "What the heck?"

Steve eyed him coolly. "Don't like to lose, do you?"

Jack breathed in deeply and, eyes narrow, shook his head.

Steve nodded and crossed to stand beside Jack. He whipped out his revolver in a flash and quickly fired six shots that hit the cans in rapid succession.

Steve eyed the horizon behind where he fired while the smoke cleared, then returned his revolver to its holster at his side.

Jack blinked and shook his head. "Amazing," he whispered. "How'd you do it?"

Steve cocked his head at Jack, a smile playing at the corner of his mouth. "Well for starters, I didn't put blanks in *my* gun."

Jack's anger rose, but quickly gave way to laughter. "Good grief. I thought I was going crazy."

"Sorry, kid. But that was an old trick your dad played on me once when I was a rookie. Let's try it again," Steve said, "this time with live ammo."

Relieved, Jack nodded, and they set to it for the next hour. Steve demonstrated the finer points of safely operating a dangerous weapon and how to use it properly when the worst happened and you're forced to shoot in order to save lives. Jack did well, learning a proper stance, grip, a smooth trigger pull, sight picture, sight alignment, draw, presentation, efficient reloads, as well as the use of cover and concealment.

Jack loved every minute of that time, except the episode with the blanks, and he imagined these would be the kinds of lessons his dad would have taught him as he grew older.

But Dad was gone, buried somewhere in the sands of Thandalia. Jack didn't know where. As they walked back to the camp, Jack asked.

"Where is my dad buried?"

"After we get through the Brothers," Steve replied, motion-ing to the two enormous rocks that loomed on the other side of camp, "there's a road that goes west to the Destronn Plain, east to the Valley of Stars, and north to Andos. He's buried near the city."

"So we won't be able to visit on this trip? I'd like to, um, pay my..." he trailed off.

"No, kid," Steve said. "But when this is over, and Michelle is safely home in Myrtle, I'll bring you there. If it's within my power at all, we will go there together."

"That's not a blank promise, is it?" Jack asked, smiling.

"No, Jack," Steve replied. "It's fully loaded."

The band was sitting around a campfire, circled up and silent while So-addan sang softly in her native Thandalian tongue. The song played sweetly on the borderlands of grief and hope, and it went to Jack's heart, though he mentally understood only the odd word here and there. Jack and Steve halted some distance away, bowing their heads. Jack thought of his father, reciting the Twenty-Third Psalm as he lay dying in this land, and he said his own prayer to the Maker of the worlds, for protection and for courage, and for every loved one back home.

"Amen," Jack said as the song ended.

Timman gazed at his daughter tenderly, his eyes shining with pride and affection. "You are the brightest star in my heaven, my love."

She smiled and crossed to embrace him. "Thank you for making it so I could come, Father. It means the world to me."

Timman returned the embrace and, closing his eyes on tears, said, "I love you, my dear. You had to come, of course. I could not leave you behind. Everything will be different after this."

"Our world will be free," she said. "We'll be able to go home."

Steve watched; then his gaze turned to Michelle, and he looked at her with such affection that Jack looked away.

Benny began serving up dinner. "Come and get it," he said, apron on and spatula in hand. "It's hot and here, so grab it and growl."

Jack stepped forward, smiling.

"Jack," Steve said, holding out a hand for him to wait. He turned to the younger man, almost eye-level with him now. "Your dad was my best friend. I loved the man. And I would do anything for Ruben Zulu's son. I hope you know that." Jack nodded and Steve continued. "But my girl comes first—before you, or me, or Wheeler, or almost anyone or anything."

"I know that, sir."

"When the trouble comes," Steve continued, "I'll be fighting for Michelle."

Wheeler called over. "Come and eat, gentlemen. Benny has cooked up something he describes as 'especially bodacious.' So, we are in for—for something."

Jack and Steve came nearer and joined the line for food. "You okay, Jack?" Benny asked.

"Same as always," Jack replied.

"That good, huh?" Benny said. "Well, I may not be a battle-tested warrior or the very best horseman ever to have joined a mission, but never forget this, man. I've got your back, Jack."

"Thanks, B," Jack said, then motioned to his mushy portion. "What is this?"

"That is some gross field rations, bro. It's what happens when Benny is given a very limited budget and supplies."

"Bodacious?" Jack asked.

"Sometimes it's all in the presentation, my friend. The power of positive reinforcement." Benny took a bite, grimaced, then gulped it down. "Wow," he called loudly. "That is some amazing grub." He leaned close to Jack and whispered. "See, it works every time."

Tytrus coughed. "Delicious grub? This tastes like actual grubs."

Benny shrugged at Jack, then called back, "Right again, Tytrus."

Chapter Eleven

The Ruins
of Balmard

The next morning they packed up camp before dawn and rode through the ancient path between the twin gigantic rocks. These behemoths shot up out of the ground to reach astonishing heights. Jack gazed up at the translucent edges of the white-hued monsters, marveling at their size and slick appearance. He edged near one on Captain Kirk, who whinnied gently as Jack ran his hand along the smooth surface.

"It's considered impious to touch the Brothers," Tytrus said, frowning.

Jack yanked his hand back. "Oh, dag. Sorry, Tytrus. I didn't mean to offend."

"Well," Tytrus replied, riding close to Jack with a stern expression, "the penalty is serious." He sucked the end of his finger, then quickly stuck it in Jack's ear. "Ha!" he said, riding ahead quickly as Jack slapped at him.

"Ah, yes!" Benny laughed, balancing better on Ozzie during this leg of the journey, "it's the ol' Wet Willy. I'm so happy to see you putting my training to good use, Tytrus."

"Master B," Tytrus replied, bowing from the saddle.

"Gross," Michelle said.

"Disgusting," So-addan agreed.

"Why can't you teach him something good from Earth?" Michelle asked. "Why do you have to share the grodiest parts of life in Myrtle?"

Benny raised his hands. "I told him the cool stuff, too."

"It's true, Princess," Tytrus replied, circling back to the group of young riders but staying clear of Jack. "I know all about Hulk Hogan, Pez dispensers, gummy bears, and the mighty Thundercats."

"See," Benny said, "he's got all the top cultural touchstones right there. Well done, my young apprentice."

Michelle sighed, muttering, "Good grief."

"And Charles Brown, too," Tytrus said, side-eying Benny for approval.

Benny puffed out his bottom lip and nodded encouragement. "I'll give you that one."

So-addan pointed ahead at the dim path. "We will show you a small wonder from our world up ahead."

They rode on, talking as they went, while the adults stayed just ahead of them. The three rangers rode point, and Tytrus—assisted by Jack—was responsible for watching the rear.

Near the final part of their journey through the Brothers, they came to a vast recess on their right. The rock wall inclined sharply, leading back to what seemed an enormous cave. Everyone stopped, gazing into the shadows.

Inside the recess an ancient town was visible in the dimness, with simple dwellings made of clay and stone along the ground and more elaborate dwellings high in the wall itself.

They reminded Jack of mud dauber nests, but instead of dry brown, these were made of the same translucent colors that were everywhere in Thandalia. Their eyes had grown used to the dim road, but here a single shaft of light from high above beamed onto the entrance of the recess, bouncing off a bed of clear stone to give the strange place a surprising light. Still, the shadows persisted. Bright stalactites hung from the cave's inclined roof, and rising stalagmites dotted the ground around the dwellings.

Tytrus drew close to Jack and the other young members of the company, speaking low. "The Ruins of Balmard. Once an ancient civilization of our ancestors, who fled from the intensity of our sun in the days before we adapted to its changes."

"It's so desolate," Jack whispered.

So-addan nodded. "It is, though some dare to visit it when they journey from, or to, Gate City. In our better days—before Rancast's party came and made war—we had the ruins secured, and children would come to learn about those ancient days. Now it's either abandoned or used as a base for thieves."

"Or worse," Tytrus added.

Timman, brow knit and face serious, motioned for everyone to move on.

Jack urged Captain Kirk ahead gently, and the compliant mustang obeyed. Benny rode ahead, really growing as a rider, with Michelle and So-addan just beyond him and between the adults. Catching a glimpse of Michelle's face, Jack saw worry there. He was about to ride up alongside her to ask what was wrong when he heard a shout from behind.

"Ride!" Tytrus cried. Jack snapped back to see shapes emerging from the shadows in the ancient city. Balmard was not so empty as it had seemed. Their movement discovered, the nearest shadow-figure, a lanky rogue in black, stepped out and fired a rifle, the cracking report echoing off the rock walls.

"Go!" Timman shouted, urging Michelle and So-addan ahead while he and Wheeler turned their mounts back. Steve's revolver was out in a flash, and he fired, sending the thin attacker spiraling down to the ground with a groan.

More bandits emerged, several armed with single-fire rifles that cracked with a burst of flame from the shadows. Jack ducked and struck Benny's horse. "Go with them!" he cried, and Benny raced ahead, trailing behind Michelle and So-addan. So-addan rode close to Michelle, her hand on her weapon, glancing all around.

Jack looked back and drew his sword. The bandits fired in bursts, then darted between rocky ruins, ever closer. Jack turned his horse's head to the fight and snapped the reins with a shout. "H'ya!"

Catching up to Wheeler, he scanned the battlefield. Wheeler had the Prism Blade free and was leaping from his horse. "Follow me, Jack!"

Jack bounded from the saddle and raced alongside the older man as he met the first foe behind a slumping ruin of stone. Wheeler hewed through the first opponent's blade, then made quick work of ending him. Jack raced in, hacking down at an enemy, whose raised rifle blocked Jack's blow. Jack kicked out and caught the man on his chin, sending him sprawling. Wheeler's blade sang out in the shadows, its rainbow edge blurring as he cut down the attackers.

The battle raged around the cavern, Steve blazing away with his revolver, accompanied by Tytrus and the other Thandalian rangers, who all fired rifles into the attackers' stronghold. These enemies weren't merely vagabond thieves; they were soldiers— no doubt part of Rancast's allies in Ghistalli's Vandal army.

A shot zipped overhead and shattered a drooping stalactite behind Jack. Another spray of shots hewed down a huge stalactite just above, and he dove aside just in time before its point smashed into the ground where he'd just been. A Vandal rushed ahead, firing as he came. Jack dodged behind a low rock shelf. He ducked as another shot rang out, then drew his dad's revolver. Steadying it on the rock, he squeezed the trigger. A burst of flame came with the gunshot's cracking blast. The Vandal spun down from the strike to his arm, slinking behind a nearby hut. Jack rose, firing at the enemy snipers in the high cave wall dwellings.

The fight intensified, with close quarter contests all around. The Vandals were being driven back, at last, retreating deeper into the caves' depths. Jack fired his final rounds, then holstered his sidearm and drew his blade once again. He dug in and rushed toward the hottest part of the fight, then stumbled and—struck by a sudden vision—fell to the ground, covering his head. He dragged in ragged breaths, his heart beating seemingly out of time. He struggled to his knees and knelt in the gap just before the battle. He closed his eyes, sweat bursting out on his brow.

In his mind he saw himself surging forward, a bright rainbow-blurring blade in his hand. *The Prism Blade? Why? Where is Wheeler?* He was not there. He was not needed. Jack strode in, leaping ahead of his fellows as he struck down the first enemy in a magnificent flourish. Darting aside, he killed a second, a third, and a fourth. On and on they came, enemy after enemy, falling in turn as Jack's unstoppable power unleashed the whirlwind on his foes. He laughed as he dashed them down, and they piled all around him in heaps, upon which he leaped and raised his blade. The king of Balmard. The grateful Thandalians brought his crown and cape, and he knew this was only the first kingdom to fall to his rule. Soon all the kingdoms in all the worlds would be his. He grinned madly.

"Jack! Jack!"

He seemed to wake from a dream, slowly losing the thread of his vision as he saw Steve standing over him. Steve looked angry. "You get hit, Jack? You dropped out right when things got thick. What happened?"

Jack looked himself over. "No, no. No, I don't think I got hit."

"Well come on, boy," Steve said, irritated. "I've got to get to Michelle."

Jack stood slowly, remnants of the nightmare—*or was it a good dream?*—still clinging to his subconscious. He saw in the dim hollow of the ruin's recess that their enemies had been routed. Wheeler was mounted again and riding off toward Michelle. Steve rode behind him, a last perplexed look back at Jack. *I was smiling when he found me. I was grinning like I was in the vision.*

Tytrus was nearby, kneeling. Jack walked over and saw the prone form of Dohlun, the ranger.

Tytrus, wiping at his eye, looked over at Jack. "He stepped in there at the last, giving us cover to finish them off. He died a hero in Thandalia, for the princess and the cause. As he would have wanted."

"I'm so sorry, Ty," Jack said, kneeling beside his friend. "I, I . . . I'm so sorry."

Soon Wheeler and Steve returned with Michelle, Benny, and So-addan. Jack helped Tytrus dig a grave for Dohlun, while Timman said the words from their service. Jack looked up, wiping sweat from his eyes, and saw Steve and Wheeler huddled in conversation at the edge of the ruins. Steve was shaking his head. Wheeler looked deeply concerned.

The solemn work ended, Jack walked off to a lonely part of the ruins. He stayed there a while, apart from the group, thinking. Worrying.

They rode on eventually, the company silent as they followed Wheeler onward. The party emerged on the other side of the Brothers, leaving the path and finding again the blinding sunlight. It took a long time adjusting, but soon Jack saw more of what he'd seen on the other side. Translucent stone jutting out from a desert landscape, with orange routes cut this way and that like veins leading to one long central road.

They took the main road and followed it for many miles, the heat beating down on them. Jack drank no water on this part of the journey. He was ashamed and uncertain and felt that punishing himself was a way to atone for his inaction. But beyond the shame of inaction, the deeper shame of what he dreamed gnawed at him. It was worse. Far worse. He was more afraid of what he might become by doing than by not doing. He hated it all, was angry at himself, and he would not drink.

High, forbidding mountains called the Nor-al loomed in the distance as they came to a crossroads. The north road continued through the wreck of a ruined village. Flames still smoldered here and there, and burned-out homes stood alongside others that were crushed. Some—all too few—seemed unscathed. There were only a few villagers there rooting through the ruins, neckerchiefs pulled up for masks against the awful fumes.

"Freston," Tytrus said, nodding, "or what's left of it."

"God save us," Wheeler said, hanging his head.

Michelle rode ahead, intent on entering the village and helping the few who remained.

"Princess, no," Timman said, "we have to carry on."

Steve rode alongside Michelle, turning back to the group. "We can help them for a little while."

Wheeler nodded, and Benny rode ahead. Jack stayed with Wheeler and Timman, while the rest began handing out water, and Benny prepared food.

Wheeler wiped his forehead. "She is a compassionate and good-hearted girl."

Timman glanced at Jack, then back at Michelle, who was kneeling by an elderly man covered in soot. She bandaged his bloodied leg while he drank from her canteen, So-addan beside her, assisting. Timman coughed. "She will need to be more than compassionate if we are to end this war. She will have to be powerful, spectacular, and deadly."

Wheeler squinted as he looked on at Michelle, who was wiping the old man's face clean with her own white sleeve. "She is never more powerful than when she is acting in love." He sighed, then looked over at Timman and Jack. "Nor are any of us."

Chapter Twelve

Jack and
the Ring of Glory

J ack watched Wheeler go, joining the others in the work to serve the remaining residents of Freston village. Jack raised his reins and urged Captain Kirk ahead. Timman rode beside him, silently staring at the devastated village.

"It's terrible, Master Timman," Jack said.

"It is."

They dismounted at the edge of town, bending near the broken remains of an archway over the village gate. Statues lay around, some half-sunk in sand and others shattered. Jack bent to gather the pieces of one, laying them in a pile near the half-faced image it seemed to belong to. "Who were they?" Jack asked, glancing over the ruined statues.

"They were the great ones from this village," Timman replied. "It's a tradition among our kind to honor our great ones with statues outside of town. It is called the ring of glory. I believe the ring of sages' statues back at the Gock is based on this Thandalian practice."

"We do it on Earth too, sometimes," Jack said, "make statues honoring greatness. I saw one of Abraham Lincoln at the state capital. He was a leader back home, a long time ago."

"I would like to see it."

"It's in Charleston," Jack said. "It's a real big city—well, big for West Virginia."

Timman sighed. "This one I know." He blew dust from the decapitated head of an elven matron's statue. "This honors Luden Kind."

"Who was she?" Jack brushed sand from another half-shattered face and placed it gently next to its broken pieces.

"A poet and an elder. She helped found Freston, along with Fressur and Dant. She wrote what we call *fin-dellohn*—poems using each letter of a person's name, to honor them. Her poems about Fressur are why we know so much about him and what he did."

"He was a hero?"

"He was. Perhaps like your Lincoln."

"Is your home near here?" Jack raised a mostly intact statue, leaned it against another, then wiped at his sweaty forehead.

"I am from that way," Timman said, pointing west. "If you follow that road, skirting the sacred forest, as we will, you will come to the Destronn Plain. I was born on the plain, in sight of Destrow itself."

"The other way is to the Valley of Stars, and north to Andos?" Jack asked.

"Yes. Well, northwest is Andos, where few have ever been and lived to tell. This crossroads is the intersection of destiny, my young acolyte."

Jack nodded, looking up at the junction of the two orange roads.

Timman continued. "That way does indeed lead to Andos. I have dreamed of going to the Golden City since I was a small child. My mentor always had such reverence for the Thaons, and he passed this on to me. 'There is nothing better than to be a god,' he would say. 'And if you cannot be a god, then get as close as you can.'" Master Timman gazed up at the purple-hued sky. "I was raised on the Destronn Plain and grew up in a small village many miles from the great city of Destrow. I used to look at its buildings in the distance and dream of being someone there. I didn't even know what they did, but I knew I wanted to be a part of it. I was an explorer, even then." He laughed, and Jack smiled.

Jack loved Master Timman's classes at the Academy. The wise older elf knew so much about Thandalia's secrets. Jack always knew he would understand more about that land, and Michelle's people's history, if he listened closely. Master Timman continued. "I made a discovery as little more than a child. I found a hoard of rare artifacts in an undiscovered chamber, including some priceless manuscripts. They were in a cave system on the outskirts of the city. So even from a young age I had wealth and fame, and I made a name for myself in and around Destrow. When I was old enough, I moved my family there, eventually becoming a scholar at the university as I continued my archeology missions. Eventually, I grew too influential for some in the district, and I was appointed to the Wayland's Academy. My own little village even made a statue of me for their ring of glory."

"Your parents must be very proud," Jack said.

"My father was," he replied. "Mother died at my birth, but Father lived many years after. He died in the war."

"Is that why you hate Rancast so much?"

Timman nodded. "Yes, Jack. It offends me that Rancast, a Vandal—meaning no offense to you, of course—has taken the fruit of the sacred tree at Andos. I hate that he was the first non-Thaon to enter the Golden City. I hate that he grew more and more powerful on our sacred food and that he, already long-lived, will now never die."

Jack spat. "He'll die when I . . . when someone . . . kills him."

"Very true, Jack," Timman replied, a fire in his eyes that Jack took for fury. "I would love for it to be me. The one who does will be . . . well, they would be in all the rings of glory across the world."

"Maybe Michelle will be the one to end him," Jack said.

"She is capable of great things," Timman replied, "as I have told her many times. No one quite knows what power she commands. She is the key—the key to it all."

Jack looked at Wheeler, who stood assisting her as she bathed the wounds of a withered old man. "She is very good."

"She can be great," Timman said. "I have instructed her in the ways of our people, and of her own destiny. She can be a weapon of doom to be used against Rancast."

"And Ghistalli," Jack said. "He's the one who's actually here."

"Rancast is not here, perhaps," Timman said bitterly, gazing around at the burned-out buildings and the villagers, all weak and wounded, "but his offensive influence is everywhere we look." He tied his huge six-legged horse to the broken remains of the city gate, then walked off toward Wheeler and Michelle.

Jack left the statues in the best shape he knew how, then

crossed to just beneath the broken arch. A heavy iron bell had plunged and sunk into the hard ground. He bent and gripped the exposed lip of the bell. He pulled, but the bell didn't budge. He wiped his brow, then bent again, this time straining with everything he had. The bell stayed where it was.

"You know who else tried to pull that bell out?"

Jack looked up to see Tytrus. "Who?"

Tytrus shook his head. "No one."

"Dumb?" Jack asked.

"Maybe," Tytrus replied. "But you're also the one who sees it's the central feature of the gateway into the village. It's a symbol of their strength. It's crucial for their festivals and the life of the village. It's prominent and important, and you, being you, wanted to fix that."

"So people would notice what I did?" Jack asked, his eyebrows knitting. "So I could have the glory of doing this important job?"

Tytrus cocked his head sideways. "I didn't say that, Jack."

Jack rose to his feet, and they stood in silence awhile, taking in the town.

"How long is the ride to Destrow?" Jack asked.

"A few days—maybe a week. It depends on how close the old-timers dare get to the forest."

"I don't know much about the forest. It's what, haunted?"

Tytrus shrugged. "They say so, yeah. Only a kind of priest can go in there, and that, only once a month. They are atoning for some great evil done."

"Done by a human," Jack said flatly.

Tytrus nodded. "More than human, yes. Rancast, of course. Our people used to go in. It was always sacred but not forbidden.

When I was toddling at my father's knee I went in with my family. We would go on pilgrimages—like holy hikes—and I would ride on my father's back. We would walk the paths, listen to the song of the doo-wairose singing from the treetops, and see the hermit shanties. I even saw one of the old hermits once. He was all green, as I recall—even his skin had changed—and seemed to be dressed in moss."

"Are you sure it wasn't just a tree?"

"I can't be certain, I guess. He was short, fat, and asked me if I had a really sharp knife he could borrow."

"Doesn't sound like a tree."

"Sounds like a weird hermit in the sacred wood of Cran-dor."

"That's the easiest explanation."

"Not super complicated," Tytrus agreed.

"So, maybe a five-day journey." Jack nodded to the water and food being handed out to the villagers. "Will we have enough to make it?"

"We packed light, so I doubt it," Tytrus said, wincing. "But we do have one less to feed."

"Was it my fault, Ty?" Jack asked, head dipping.

"Don't say that, Jack."

Jack toed the bell, still not looking up. "Did you see me—at the ruins? I stayed on the ground."

"Head up, Jack." Tytrus lifted Jack's chin with a firm fist. "I saw you fighting. I saw you shooting. I know you. You're a fighter—a brave fighter. I'm glad you're with us. Let's not lose sight of this opportunity. We might be close to ending this war. Don't lose heart, Jack. The pivotal moments are ahead of us. And you always shine when the contest is on the line."

Jack smiled at his friend, but inside, he heard another voice. *Of course I'll show up when glory's there to be grasped. What all great men do. That's what he does. That's what I do.*

Chapter Thirteen

The
Best Move

J ack patted his horse, growing fonder every day of the sturdy animal. The Earth horses, having been given the same medicine he and the other Myrtle residents took, were adapting well to the Thandalian sand and sun. The forest always on their right, they rode over a wide open landscape, dotted with pale scrub brush and crisscrossed with orange paths around towering rock formations that rose and fell like a dragon's spine in the distance. They never came closer than a few miles to Cran-dor Forest and edged away farther at night. The road they traveled was called the Highway of Light, an ancient route that circled the sacred forest.

Jack rode close to Wheeler one evening as they moved farther away before making camp. "What happened in Cran-dor?"

"Well, Jack," Wheeler replied, "Rancast used the forest in a brutal way, not paying homage to the Maker upon entry and exit, nor showing the proper humility by kneeling at every stream to clean his hands. He did not observe the rites. His filthy army tore through, knowing no sacred thing but their will and their appetites. They burned hermit villages and murdered pilgrims in the sacred streams. They burned whole groves of fruit trees and built weapons from the forest to aid their assault on Andos."

"Aren't there keepers of the forest?" Jack asked. "I read about them once—the Stewards of the Black Blade?"

"There are, now."

"Because of..."

Wheeler nodded. "Because of the impiety of Rancast and his men. This is but one of the many marks against him and all Vandals."

"It makes sense why it was hard for them to accept me."

"There is a context to their mistrust, even if it is not always just. The forest is actually sacred, a thin place in many ways. I long to walk again its ancient paths. It is a place for holy ceremonies. Some exchanged vows there in the old days."

Jack looked over at Wheeler, then to the forest. After a little while, he said, "It's beautiful."

"Stay away, Jack. There is a spirit in that forest, and it is deeply displeased with Vandals. Do not put it to the test. And the Stewards watch."

Jack nodded. "Yes, sir." It was the last place he ever wanted to visit.

They camped again, then rode out the next morning. They crossed the mighty Telvar River at a low place by an old bridge, and continued on through the Enlay Valley.

Ever rising as they left the valley behind, the landscape changed and each day the temperature dropped a little more. On the fourth day, as they crested the edge of the Destronn Plain, they gazed at the distant skyline of the city Destrow, so recently a captured prize of the Vandal revolutionary forces.

Now it had been liberated by the outnumbered forces of Captain Bon-hadden and was controlled by the Thandalian loyalist army. Beyond the city, impossibly high cliffs rose out of the plain like great bats' wings on the far side, their heights seeming to brood over the city. These were the Lika Mountains, and Jack was told they were made up of the same translucent stone seen all over Thandalia so far on their journey, but they seemed only shadows at this distance. Many villages and some small towns lay along the orange road in the distance between them and Destrow.

Michelle squinted, pointing toward the city. "Will we come to it tomorrow?"

"Yes, Princess," Timman replied. "Tomorrow evening."

She nodded. "Are they being cared for, the citizens? Have we rallied around them? Is everything that can be done being done?"

"It's all in motion," Timman said, pointing. "See there, the dust rising up from that road outside the city? Well, you cannot see the road, but there is a wide one there to the south. The dust kicks up from our caravans in action. The free cities have been bringing supplies and doctors, and every kind of volunteer has been pouring in since the victory. Destrow will have more of the army and the volunteer services within its walls than many other places combined."

"The rangers are there," Tytrus said, gazing through his binoculars. "They secured every high turret around the city. I have no idea how they ever achieved it with the guns that had been mounted there by Ghistalli's Vandal forces. Captain Bon-hadden is a genius."

"He is that. A true martial tactician, and an old friend," Wheeler said. "I would not have believed it possible—this legendary feat—were it not for him. What he has done here is a miracle, so it is."

"Ghistalli must be fuming," Timman said. "I should like to see his face after this catastrophe for their side. He has likely killed half his lieutenants."

Tytrus growled. "I hope he has."

They rode on. Benny, now grown very comfortable on Ozzie, came alongside Jack, and they rode a little ways apart from the rest. "How's my best friend doing?"

"Good, B," Jack replied. "How's my best friend doing?"

"Solid."

Jack looked across, a wave of gratitude washing over him. "Benny, you're crushing it with the meals on this trip. What you did at Freston was so cool. And making our food stretch these last few days? Amazing. Dude, it reminded me what kind of guy you are. You don't need the spotlight." He looked off at the distant city.

"Mama mia, Jack," Benny said. "If you love me, just say so."

"I've got your back, B," Jack replied with a grin, then shook his head. "Doesn't have the ring like when you say it."

"I've got what you lack, Jack," Benny replied, "a best friend with an easy-to-rhyme name."

Jack laughed, shrugging. "I've got your penny, Benny?"

Benny shook his head. "Terrible. I've got your enemy, Ben-en-y?"

"Even worse," Jack said. "I've got it. I've got your banjo, my dear friend, Benito."

"Oh man, that's the worst!" Benny said, cackling so hard that he almost slid off Ozzie. "Okay, okay," he went on, "this is the one. I'll strike the deathblow, my handsome friend Benito.

Yeah, use that."

Jack nodded at Ozzie. "I've got your palomino, Benny Marino?"

Benny waved his hands. "Nope, that's so bad. And Ozzie's an appaloosa, not a palomino. Duh."

"Oh, I forgot," Jack said, "that my best friend was a world-renowned horses scholar."

Benny took on an air of sophistication. "We say 'horses genius' in the profession. A horses scholar is a vulgar term. It's like calling my father a pizza guy instead of what he is, an *Italiano Maestro Cuisiner.* Fie on your 'horses scholar' balderdash!"

"My horse's color isn't balderdash," Jack replied, feigning offense, "it's golden."

"Your horse's collar is dirty," Benny retorted snobbishly. "Needs a good cleaning. Got ring around the horse's collar."

Jack wheezed, breathed in deep, and took a quick drink from his canteen. He looked over at Benny. "I've got your back, bro."

"I know," Benny said. "But don't worry about me. I know you're focused on Michelle—on taking care of her. And I'm with you. She's got a lot on her magical shoulders—the hopes of a whole world, really— and I want to help you help her."

"Thanks, B."

"I know this is complicated for you, Jack. I know it's not easy being what you are when she is who she is. Both of you have these expectations for yourselves that are out of this world—literally. And then there's everyone else's expectations piled on. It's gotta be super hard for both of you."

Jack nodded. "Part of it, for me, is that I don't want to live up to some expectations."

"Oh, like being another Rancast?"

Jack blew out a deep breath. "Yeah, to get straight to the point. Yeah. I don't want to be like him."

"You aren't, man," Benny said, shaking his head.

"I'm trying not to be." Jack blinked and glanced over at Michelle, reaching inside his shirt for the pawn hanging from its chain. "Sometimes the best move on the chess board is not to move at all."

Chapter Fourteen

Destrow's Welcome

The company came to Destrow Hollow Road, a route riven between the Lika Mountains and not far from the city. They met a small company of soldiers there and Tytrus and the two remaining Thandalian rangers rode ahead with them, not making the last camp with the rest of the company. So it was only seven who, the next afternoon, approached the city. Michelle was exuberant, riding alongside a silent Master Timman.

"See how they fill the city!" Michelle called back, pointing to the road that ran, like theirs, toward the city gate. The main road was thick with traffic. Soldiers marched in, swelling the army there. Equipment, weapons, and supplies of every kind flooded in, along with volunteers. The city wall featured many high narrow towers, all flying the Thandalian standard. Below the parapets, teeming with elven soldiers, the wall gaped open at its great gate. Jack's heart stirred to see it.

"It is a glorious sight, is it not?" Wheeler asked.

Jack could hardly find words and muttered, "Amazing."

They rode nearer. At the point where the roads converged,

they left their horses. It was a mile from the city in a modest corral operated by bowing elven children. The animals were led to a small yellow barn by the oldest children, while the young ones gaped at Michelle. From there, they walked, and Jack stretched, glad to be out of the saddle.

An exultant crowd met them as they reached the last half-mile before the gates. The incoming roads were temporarily blocked off, and the trail of supplies and people was halted.

Michelle grinned at the joy all around but glanced over at the halted supplies with a quick look of concern. "They must not stop for us."

"On the contrary, they must," Wheeler said, walking up behind her. "It is right that you should be seen and celebrated, Princess. That is what we came here to do. You are inspiring them. Let them be inspired. Be what you are. Be who you are."

She nodded, swallowing hard. "I'll do my best."

Timman, eyes thinning to slits, peered at the gates and high turrets. "I hope all is secure. We cannot fail here." He walked just behind and to Michelle's right as they progressed. He smiled wide and began waving.

Jack frowned, thinking Master Timman should fall back farther, like the rest had. If anyone should walk so close, it should be Wheeler, or even Steve. But it was Master Timman's home, Jack remembered, and this must mean the world to him to return this way. The enraptured Thandalians, many who had certainly suffered from the years-long occupation of the city, lined the road approaching the gate.

They threw flowers into the road, calling, "The Last Thaon! Princess of Light!"

Michelle held her head high and smiled warmly, waving

in a dignified style and taking care especially to notice and acknowledge the many children who waved wildly at her. They knelt when she was directly in line with them, so that a wave of reverent homage followed her as she approached, surrounded by a contrasting ecstatic overflow of joy.

Reverence. Exuberance. A pious delight.

Steve scanned the crowd, his hand close to his revolver and his eyes, like Timman's, thinned to slits and scanning every direction.

"The Last Thaon! Light and Hope has come! Princess of Andos!" they cried.

Timman saluted as many called out, "Timman of Destrow! Our soon and certain sage, Great Timman, Guide of the Lightflyer!" and other praises. Jack remembered how long it had been since Timman was even in Thandalia, let alone his own home region. A twinge of jealousy sprouted in Jack's heart, and he worked to fight it back. He didn't want to be the kind of person who envied what Timman was experiencing.

Attempting to focus on his duty, Jack scanned the crowd to spy out any threat to Michelle. But soon his attention wavered, and he found that he had been looking to see if any in the crowd were shouting for him. Some were, and his chest rose in response.

"A Waylander! A hero for the Wayland and every world!" cried a pocket of Wayland Academy students, no doubt there to volunteer in the city's relief. Their uniforms were like Jack's, and he recognized some from the Gock. Jack's crisp open-collared white shirt was tucked into his barley-colored pants, his blue jacket open in the heat. The young girls in the group screamed, and the boys shouted, "Jack Zulu, a hero for our cause!"

Jack smiled and nodded, his head dropping in a display of modesty he didn't really feel. He felt sadness when they neared the gates, sorry this procession was over. Hungry for more. But inside the gates, the celebration went on and intensified.

The streets of the strange city were lined like an old parade of champions he had seen on TV for sports teams. The elven citizens cheered and sang as Michelle came in sight. People hung over balconies, waving madly and tossing flowers in the road. Rhythmic music boomed out as they crossed the threshold of the city. The buildings seemed fashioned to imitate the natural landscape, with translucent towers and purple and orange-hued stone all around, decorated with streamers and flags. Jack even saw enormous murals stretching up into the sky, depicting Michelle with wings flung wide, light pulsing from her edges. These were often attached at great heights to high balloons, like Earth's hot air balloons Jack had seen in pictures, with arcing tops that rode the high, hot winds of Thandalia. The balloons seemed to fill the sky above the city, and below them in their baskets were more thrilled Thandalians, launching vibrant blooms over the sides and cheering. Several of the balloons, much more mobile than those from Earth, zipped around the city heights trailing banners bearing Thandalian script and images of Michelle, Timman, and even Jack in a few places.

Tytrus and the other two rangers rejoined the party there, alongside a more robust guard that surrounded and guided them through the city streets. Many of these soldiers bore the standard of Captain Bon-hadden, a Thandalian bird called the swooping skite. It hung even from some of the balconies and balloons. Tytrus saw Benny eyeing the high balloons. "We call them sky sliders."

Benny, wearing his "Myrtle, West Virginia, a good town with a nice, old bridge" shirt, shot him a thumbs-up. "We call them hot air balloons."

"Ever been in one?" Tytrus asked.

"Yeah, buddy," Benny replied. "Cincinnati, 1976. Picture a young red-headed child in jean shorts clambering up—"

Wheeler coughed and nodded ahead. "Perhaps we could save the scintillating Cincinnati story for a better time, Benito?"

Benny nodded, playing off his deep blush. "Right you are, Wheeler. Guys," he said to Tytrus and his ranger fellows, pointing two fingers to his eyes, then out toward the crowd, "let's lock it in and stay focused here. Eyes up and chests out and teeth set and feet at the kick-ready. Be ready to kick, guys. Get those kickers oiled up and ready. This ain't story time, fellas."

Tytrus grinned and turned back to scanning for threats.

Drums rumbled from far back in the crowd, and a chorus of deep masculine voices sang out in a triumphant chorus. Jack felt it in his gut, and he wiped at his eyes. Then the higher-pitched harmonies of thousands of elven ladies joined in, and the song swelled into a kind of ethereal anthem of hope the likes of which Jack had never imagined.

"Sook-uh, lun-a, tam bray hone! Ha-la naad eeyayo lune!"

They sang, and their song soared on high and split the sky, spraying around them a warm glow of joy, with a wispy hint of earnest longing. Jack felt more than he could comprehend, and he thought of his own home, his mother, funerals, weddings, and the national anthem before a baseball game. With his less-than-elementary Thandalian, he couldn't translate fast enough in his mind, but he heard words for glory, for joy, and, of course, for light and hope.

Jack glanced over, saw tears streaking down Tytrus's face, and saw his mouth open as he sang along with the exuberant joy. Wheeler gazed wistfully around, eyes shining. Benny nodded his head, eyes half-closed above a wide smile. Timman's back was to Jack, but Jack knew this meant the world to every Thandalian. So-addan wept as she sang, and she struggled to keep her composure as occasional sobs overtook her. They all knew their part in the anthem, and the masculine and feminine blended across the city to form a strange harmonic masterpiece that was far more precise than the near-shouts Jack often heard during events on Earth that involved singing. It was a form of music unfamiliar to Jack, but beautiful, nonetheless. All around, the Thandalians wept and sang. This went on for several blocks, with a new song starting up as soon as the last one faded, until they turned a last bend in the road.

Jack gazed up at a high tower, flat on top with high buildings surrounding it and a vast open square below. It was the center of town. The high tower. Where Michelle was, he knew, set to address her people tomorrow. It was not so high as the blue tower back in the Wayland, but it was impressive.

As the procession reached its end at what Jack recognized as the House of Thandal, the crowd grew more sober. His heart sank as he saw that the gold and white sanctuary had been badly damaged. Ghistalli's occupation had meant desecration on top of depravation.

As they approached the gates of the sacred site, Jack moved closer to Michelle. Timman, stretching his legs, turned to Michelle, and Steve walked up beside them both, along with Wheeler. Jack heard the conversation, as the near crowd had fallen into a reverent silence.

"Princess Bright," Timman said, "I advise that my kinsmen and I accompany you ahead to pay your respects. The citizens will appreciate your piety. They will wait to hear from you tomorrow in the square."

Michelle nodded. "The Rite of Grief must be for the eventide, but as the sun dips beyond the mountains, the Festal Revel is signaled by the lighting of the tower."

"It is, Princess," Timman answered, clearly pleased at her knowledge. "Many will feast and dance and make merry tonight, though properly and without excess. Then at noon tomorrow, you will address them in the square, which will signal a turn toward the crucial work of ending this war and recapturing all that has been stolen from us."

Michelle inhaled deeply. "Let's go to the House of Thandal and grieve these terrible days. Then we will give thanks to our Creator, Sustainer, and Deliverer."

"Amen," Steve whispered.

Timman bowed, then led the way inside the courtyard. Tytrus and So-addan followed behind Timman and Michelle, and other Thandalians met them, bowing low to the young Thaon princess.

Wheeler stayed behind, alongside Jack and Benny, while Steve strayed to the gate, his eyes on his daughter.

"I should not worry about the rite, Steve," Wheeler said. "It is important she honors their customs, but there is nothing in them to conflict with her faith."

Steve turned a moment and fixed Wheeler with a significant stare. "I'm not worried about her faith. I'm worried about her safety."

Wheeler nodded. "She is not safe anywhere, Steve. None of

us are. But we all chose this risk, knowing what it might mean."

Steve nodded, turning back with eyes squinting into the distance as Michelle entered the House of Thandal.

She returned in half an hour, accompanied by a plainly dressed elven man who looked to be in his seventies. He was thin and muscular, pale-skinned, his silver hair cut short. His face bore many scars, and he limped along, aided by a cane. He was speaking intensely with Michelle, and Steve's hand strayed toward his sidearm. Timman seemed to try to intervene between them, but the scarred old man stepped closer to Michelle and crowded Timman out.

"What's happening?" Steve asked.

Wheeler, who had been speaking with a Thandalian elder, turned back. "It is him."

Benny scowled. "Him who?"

Jack recognized the figure from pictures and descriptions. "That's Captain Bon-hadden, the hero of the city's recapture."

Benny's nose scrunched up. "He looks like . . . well, not like a hero."

Wheeler stepped closer. "He has no doubt been fasting since the victory. Praying for the safety and victory of our cause. He is a devout man, and humble, yes. He is not from any city. He is from what we would call in Myrtle 'the sticks.'"

Benny chuckled, "Myrtle is the sticks, and so is all of West Virginia, really."

Wheeler nodded. "Then we should get along very well with the captain, to be sure."

Steve's brow knit. "Why's he hounding my girl?"

Wheeler peered at the approaching group. "Notice, Steve, that he does not touch her. His is a respectful position. He simply situates himself where no other can interpose."

Steve gave a grunt. "I'll interpose him."

"He is Thandalia's greatest warrior," Wheeler said, "so take care."

The party arrived at the gate, and Wheeler bowed, introducing everyone. Jack saw that Michelle noticed her father's distress, and he admired her when she crossed to take his hand, holding it as the formal introductions went on.

Michelle interjected when it came to Steve.

"Father," she said, bowing to Steve, "may I introduce you to Captain Bon-hadden, a noble hero of our cause?"

"Of course," Steve replied. "I'm pleased to meet you, Captain."

"Thank you, Chief Robinson," Bon-hadden replied. "The honor is mine. Your daughter is brave to come, sir. I counseled against it, of course, but I was, I see now, overruled."

"You advised against it?" Steve asked, surprise plain. Wheeler frowned.

Timman stepped forward, frustration clear. "We have much to sort out and discuss. But the princess has been traveling for many days and needs to rest. We must see to her accommodation—"

Bon-hadden interrupted, "I have secured an apartment not far from here for her and her company."

Timman frowned. "She is a Thaon, Captain—the last Thaon. She cannot be housed in an apartment. Her accommodation will be at the palace."

"I know who she is," Bon-hadden replied. "I know it very well. The palace is where Becker Ghistalli himself stayed, as did the other Vandal tyrants of this city, for years. You have not been here in a long time, I fear. It is honeycombed with secret passages and traps. I didn't even set up my command center there. I advise, in fact I insist, as military commander of this city, that the princess be kept away from the palace and in the apartment I have selected."

Timman bristled. "I am assistant to the sage of this world, a deputy and consul of the realms. I have made preparations at the palace. My attaché has overseen the securing of the palace since last week."

Bon-hadden's eyes narrowed. "Your attaché is a haughty academic scrubling of a child and, as of a week ago, not in communication with command here."

"How dare you?" Timman asked. "I have traveled these lands with the princess, securing her safety all along the way. And now you choose to take it upon yourself to—"

"Gentlemen, please," Wheeler said, stepping forward. "We all want the same thing. Let us discuss this in private."

"In privacy where?" Tytrus asked, eyeing the crowd gathered around. It had dissipated significantly, but still hundreds loomed nearby.

Michelle looked back and forth, then swallowed hard. Raising her head, she looked at the leaders. "My father will decide where I stay."

Wheeler nodded, as Timman and Bon-hadden looked on.

Steve eyed both men, then glanced around. Finally, he spoke. "I'm sorry, Master Timman, but the palace sounds like a nightmare for security. Let's go to the captain's apartment. If it doesn't fit the bill, we'll reevaluate. But he's been on the ground here, and that means a lot."

Timman bowed, nodding his head. "We must keep her safe, no matter what. It all depends upon her." His voice was raw with passion. "We can end this horrible war. We can finish it! If only she will be all that she can be."

Jack stole a glance at Michelle, saw her blink and breathe in deeply and the corner of her eyes wrinkle. "I will do all I can for our people."

Chapter Fifteen

Getting Loosed and Juiced

Jack didn't like the apartment complex. Or, he didn't like the glorified closet that he and Benny were assigned.

Benny stretched out and kicked at Jack's shoe. "Your sneakers are blocking my path."

Jack snatched it up and placed them both on a shelf alongside his sword and backpack. "When do you think they'll get our clothes back to us?"

In T-shirts and jeans, the boys sat on the floor of the tiny half-room, barely long enough for Jack to fully stretch out. Sitting opposite each other, Benny raised his toes toward Jack. "Do my feet still stink after that sorry excuse for a shower we just had?"

"Yes!" Jack gagged, pushing the scrawny pair of pale feet away. "A little soldier's bath isn't gonna cure those dogs. You need, like, a vat of molten lava to fix that stench."

Benny frowned. "The dogs are what they are, I guess. You hungry?"

Jack sighed. "Same answer as twenty minutes ago, B. I'm not that hungry, but I will be again. We'll get some grub tonight, I'm pretty sure."

"What if we go find it?" Benny asked.

"I think he wants us to stay closer," Jack said. "Michelle might need me . . . .us."

"Who wants us to stay closer?" Benny asked, a skeptical expression on his face. "Who exactly is in charge right now? Whose orders do we follow? Is it Timman, who got knocked down a couple pegs earlier? Or is it Bon-hadden, who seems to be in charge of everyone and also constantly worried that everyone isn't doing what he wants all the time? Or is it Steve, who Michelle defers to? Is it Michelle—the last Thaon herself and with whom I was in a play in third grade where she played the part of—wait for it—a princess, and I played a bale of hay?" Benny scratched his chin. "Is it Wheeler?"

Jack raised his open hands. "I think I was a donkey in that one. As for who's in charge? Not sure. I guess it's Wheeler. He's our master, after all. That means something."

"Yeah," Benny agreed. "But what if Steve asked you to do something for Michelle, and Wheeler told you to do something else?"

Jack exhaled slowly. "I guess it would depend on what it was."

"You don't have the facts in this case. You just have to act on their commands."

Jack didn't get to answer because a knock was heard and Tytrus strode in, So-addan behind him. "This room is even smaller than mine," Tytrus said, laughing.

So-addan peeked over his shoulder. "Not quite the hero's quarters, huh, Jack?"

Jack smirked.

"You're cramped in here like sardines, I see," Tytrus said,

wrinkling his nose. "But it smells much worse."

Benny stood up. "Jack has a foot odor issue."

Jack rose, shaking his head. "Yeah, and Benny's as tall as Magic Johnson."

So-addan made a gagging noise. "I wish this wizard son of John could purify the air in here."

"Help us, Magic Johnson." Tytrus pinched his nose. "We are going to procure some real Thandalian food—and meet a contact of mine. Want to come along?"

Benny clapped his hands. "You bet your pointy ears, we do."

So-addan turned to Jack. "Coming?"

"Can you just leave her?" Jack asked.

So-addan sagged a little. "She's safer than she's been in a long time, Jack. Even Father sees that now. He and Captain Bon-hadden are working out the security arrangements for tomorrow. She is resting. Her father is just outside her door. There are so many guards. She is fine, Jack. You need to relax and see a little bit of the city."

"You're probably right," he replied. "Thanks. I just need to check in with Wheeler."

After a quick consultation with his master, he joined the young company, and they made their way through a twisting labyrinth of corridors and back and forth through secret paths and passageways. Jack had no idea where he was or how they would get back. But he trusted Tytrus to guide them.

They issued at last into an alley and walked quickly to the street it fed into, joining a crowd that walked along the paved roadway. This was a clean garden area. Signs of the occupying army's destruction were present, but what it had been, and would be again, was visible. It made Jack feel hopeful. Looking up, he saw the tower with the flat top. It loomed ahead, and he saw that security was swarming around its base. They hurried on. Soon, they doubled back and walked for another thirty minutes till they reached a rundown part of town, with hooded figures peering suspiciously at them from hollow eyes that glanced nervously around.

"Get juiced?" a skinny figure in a black cloak asked, flashing a tube of translucent green ooze quickly, then secreting it back into his sleeve. "Get juiced?"

"No," Tytrus said, firmly but quietly.

Benny opened his mouth, a puzzled expression on his face, but So-addan shook her head. "Not now."

Again and again, off-looking characters flashed them similar tubes and asked if they wanted to get juiced. Tytrus always declined, and they carried on until they came to a kind of café.

Jack and Benny waited outside with So-addan, while Tytrus hurried inside and joined the line waiting to order food.

"Why here?" Jack asked quietly.

So-addan glanced around, then whispered back casually, "This is Kwayrvo, a run-down black-market area. Ty brought us here because he loves the food, and he has a connection to an agent here."

"What's the juice they keep talking about?" Jack asked.

"I don't know," she replied, "but you can bet it's not good. I've heard rumors."

"Is it about Rancast's powers?" Jack asked.

"Yes." So-addan nodded to the door, where Tytrus was beckoning them in. "We'll talk inside."

Inside, they sat in a corner booth of a hazy hall, a roiling cloud of smoke hanging about the ceiling and drifting all around the room, added to by puffing patrons at nearly every booth. Tytrus showed a paper to the attendant, and their food appeared, a sizzling meat called *silwyn* topped with a purple sauce and slices of what turned out to be a peppered gourd called *sayunyas*. Benny dug in ferociously, and Jack took a cautious bite. The meat was tender and the vegetables tasty. The purple sauce added a sweetness that cut against the savory dish. Eating with relish, So-addan prompted Tytrus about the juice the vagrants had been offering.

"It's a drug," Tytrus said, wiping his mouth with a cloth napkin. "It was introduced by Ghistalli's army, of course. It's a synthetic variety drug—highly addictive—one you can get just about anywhere, but especially easily here in Kwayrvo. It claims to be the stuff that Ghistalli himself uses, a derivation of that fruit Rancast took from the sacred tree in Andos. Some say it's made from Rancast's own blood."

"Rancast once showed me a golden vial," Jack said, "and he claimed it would cure Mom. It did work. It cured Mordok of his wounded arm. It grew right back from a stump to . . . to all healed and restored."

Benny chuckled low, chewing a big bite. "And you chopped it right off again," he said, mouth full.

Jack puffed out a breath, remembering that intense battle. "But this stuff they've been showing us is green."

Tytrus nodded. "Yeah, it's all fake. These are lowlifes trying to trick visitors with a cheap addictive drug. But I think Ghistalli has been using the real thing, getting stronger." He laid down his napkin, a disgusted look on his face. "He tortured people here. His forces took kids, girls, and they spared no one, soldier or civilian. They killed the elderly. They killed anyone they saw and celebrated when they did."

"How can anyone follow him?" Benny asked, revolted. "How can he have any support?"

Tytrus inhaled deeply. "I don't know, Benny. Why do any people support such men? They are lied to about what liberation and freedom mean, about what makes for a victim and what makes an oppressor. But they defied him in this city. They did not go along—not the majority of them."

"And he slaughtered them," So-addan said, wiping at her eyes. "He enslaved and murdered and celebrated in the streets that the city was now free."

"That is Rancast's way," Jack said, a snarl on his face. "Or at least it's the result. The way of death."

Tytrus swallowed a bite and sipped his water. "My contact in this den of crime sent me a note, asking for a meeting here."

Glancing around the room at the foggy haze and the shady booths, Benny grimaced. "This place makes me queasy."

Jack glanced down at Benny's empty plate. "I see it hasn't dampened your appetite."

Benny nodded, wiping his mouth. "That was delicious, Tytrus. Five stars. I'd like to speak to the chef," he went on, eyeing the kitchen carefully, "but it looks like a good place to be murdered, so, on second thought, I'll pass."

"Captain Bon-hadden has his hands full in this city," Tytrus said. "Everything seems to be building to a moment. Tomorrow is key."

So-addan looked out the window and sighed. "Ghistalli's shadow seems to still hang over the city's edges, especially in a place like this."

Tytrus nodded. "There are thousands in jail, accused of collaborating with Ghistalli. The ones who were in jail are out and the ones out are in. And then there are the mysterious ones in the middle. Almost all side with the princess and the cause, no question. We saw that earlier. But the tyrant's lies are still rattling around in the heads of many on the margins. He promises so much. The trials of those who collaborated with Ghistalli are ongoing. There are so many cases that fifteen judges have come from the free lands to hear the cases, and their trials are being expedited. Still, lots of his sympathizers creep in the shadows."

A menacing voice sounded out of the dark hallway. "Ranger Tytrus, you and your companions are under arrest."

Chapter Sixteen

Assassin's Scheme

Jack swiveled back, hand darting to his blade.

"Easy there, hero." An elven man stepped forward, holding something aimed at Tytrus. Jack blinked. It was a bottle of purple sauce, and the man was grinning behind it. "I'm not afraid to use this."

Tytrus sprang up. *"Banda, fenna-ho ah lean somun fray!"* The two friends embraced. Jack relaxed.

"Friends," Tytrus said, returning to English and motioning to the stranger as they sat down, "this is Banda, my old friend from the Gock, a few years before your time."

"Hello," Banda said, shaking hands with Jack and Benny, then turning to hug So-addan. *"So-addan, humma don, fressta mane?"*

So-addan glanced at Jack, then slapped at Banda playfully. *"Nor-uh, don, simwitter-doney."*

Banda raised his hand in a gesture of surrender. *"Da-laan, So."*

Tytrus grinned, then turned to Jack and Benny. "Banda's been like another cousin to So-addan and me. He was a couple of years ahead of me at the academy, and he always looked out for So-addan. He went ahead of me into the Rangers—was my sponsor when I joined up."

"And you've done very well," Banda said, raising Tytrus's glass in salute, then drinking from it. "*Shacko-dun*, what is this?" he asked, his face twisting.

"It's good," Tytrus said, snatching it back. "I see your taste buds haven't recovered from getting scalded in Daylogaan."

Banda winced. "Now that was painful." He watched as Tytrus reenacted Banda drinking something he apparently wasn't supposed to and immediately regretting it. They laughed as Tytrus mimed out the event.

Jack smiled. He took to Banda right off, was drawn to his energy and playfulness. It was unusual for a Thandalian to be this kind of confident. Was it brash? He searched for a better word. *Flashy?* Maybe that was it.

"To business, I'm afraid," Banda said. "I have to report back soon." He glanced from Jack and Benny to Tytrus and So-addan. "You trust these two?"

"Yes, Banda," So-addan said quickly.

"With our lives, your life," Tytrus affirmed, "with the world."

Banda nodded. "That's good enough for me. Listen, Ty, I'm embedded with some very bad characters. I'm a pilot and an engineer, and I got in with these shadow men trying to buy discarded paracopter parts from the rebels who remained after Ghistalli's retreat."

"What's a paracopter?" So-addan asked.

"A small usually one-person flyer they use to move quickly. Can't easily get very far, but it's deadly at short distances. They had lots of them in the city during the occupation, and I have been studying their parts to try to build some for us or repair the ones we captured. It could help us in the war."

"I wonder if that's what Dunny saw at his village—at Freston," Tytrus said. "He said they attacked from the sky, like evil Thaons."

"It's bad," Banda replied. "But listen, I have to pass this through you. My own access point has gone silent on me. Maybe he got taken out. But please send word to your father," he said, nodding at So-addan. "Please tell Sage Timman—or Consul Timman, I suppose, for now—that an attack on the princess is expected tomorrow night after dark. This will be after her speech at the gathering, when confidence and goodwill is high, and the guard around her might be more relaxed. They know where she is and will attack with force. There is real Juice, and Rancast's agents have it. It's not the exact thing Rancast uses, but it's a cocktail of temporary enhancements, and the assassins are going to be given some. This will make them quick, strong, extremely violent, and very hard to kill. They have lots of inside agents—and we've verified some of them—and they will kill Timman and take the princess away. They want her," he began, then looked down.

"What?" Benny asked, jaw set.

"They want to experiment on her," Banda said. "They want to extract her blood and see what magic might be in there that Rancast can use to enhance himself even more. And then," he paused again.

Jack's lip twisted. "Then he'll add her to his trophies of conquest, his line of wives from every world."

Benny gazed up at Jack, then looked to the others, who wore somber expressions. "He'll what?"

So-addan cleared her throat. "It's what he does, Benny. Rancast has alliance marriages with royalty from nearly every one of the twelve realms. He's a monster, yes, but a politician as well. He's making a legal case for his lordship over all the worlds."

"It's true," Banda said. "And we can't let that happen. So, after the speech and the parties tomorrow, I'll join you all at the apartments. During the night tonight, I'm going to neutralize several threats in my duty zone. Others will do the same. We hope to chop off the serpent's head before it strikes."

"But this thing has lots of heads," Tytrus said warily.

"A hydra," Jack said. "You cut off one head of that monster, and another two grow in its place."

Banda blew out a low whistle. "Vandalia sounds like a terrifying place."

Benny nodded. "And the Soviets have nukes." Jack punched him. Benny rubbed his arm. "Commie-bombs aren't scary? You weren't at school last week, dude. We did a drill where we got under our desks in case of nuclear attack. Like, I'm under my desk and the ICBM—that's an intercontinental ballistic missile," here he looked at Tytrus and Banda, "hits the school. Great. Thanks, desk. It's a scary world, and sometimes all you've got is a desk."

Tytrus frowned, then turned back to Banda. "We'll be ready. What can we do tonight?"

Banda rose, eyeing the door in quick sidelong glances. "Just stay alert, and get some rest tonight. You'll need it the next few days."

"Light and hope, Banda," Tytrus said, "and may the stars meet over us again."

Banda inhaled deeply, glanced one last time at the door, then back to the group. "It will be either light or darkness tomorrow, hope or despair. There is no middle ground. This week will see the end of this war, one way or the other."

Chapter Seventeen

Quarry in the Quarry

Jack followed Tytrus and So-addan as they led the way back toward the apartment. Benny ambled along, distracted by the street vendors—especially those frying strange foods on grills along the sidewalks. Jack was eager to get back to Michelle. Even if he couldn't see her, and he doubted he would be allowed to this night before her massively important appearance, he wanted to be close by. A feeling of certainty grew inside him that he, and he alone, could protect Michelle. He felt that he must return quickly and that they all needed to be close and careful and ready. This feeling had intensified with Banda's news. Even knowing when the attack was planned for—the following night—didn't make him relax. He had to get back now.

They came into a large square on the edge of the seedy neighborhood they had eaten in. It was a busy place, with preparations for the celebration the next day in full swing. In one corner, a brightly dressed woman sold banners and long ribbons. Another stall featured instruments—mostly drums of animal skins stretched over small barrels. The largest was the balloon vendor, with small arced sky sliders—that's what Tytrus had called them—hovering overhead. Eager Thandalians were paying to join the baskets of the bigger ones for prime viewing of the princess tomorrow, and others seemed to be renting the use of smaller sliders for themselves for the same reason. They had everything from the larger more traditional hot air balloons, like the one Benny had talked about riding in once in Cincinnati, all the way down to smaller, more dynamic and steerable balloons.

"How bad would it be for me to hang out here a bit?" Benny asked.

Tytrus stopped, glanced back and forth, waited for a pair of Juice hawkers to pass, then spoke quietly. "So-addan, can you get Jack back the way we came?" She nodded, and he went on. "Then I'll stay out and do a little roaming of my own. I'll be back to get you in an hour, Benny. Stay in this square."

Benny saluted. "Aye-aye, Cap'n."

"Jack, you okay to go back?" Tytrus asked.

"Of course," he replied, feeling some frustration that Tytrus and Benny were okay to stay out after what they'd just heard. "I just don't want to wander around out here while Michelle's in danger."

Tytrus frowned. "Okay, Jack. We'll see you later on."

Jack nodded curtly and walked off, not waiting for So-addan or saying anything else.

So-addan caught up and matched his pace. "You know where you're going?"

"Not really."

"But you're headed there fast," she said. When he didn't reply, she went on. "I get it. You want to be nearby what's most important. Near her."

Jack walked on, dodging an old drunk who stumbled by. Then the intoxicated man pitched forward and rammed Jack, forcing close contact. Jack felt the point of a dagger and he spun away, kicking out and connecting with the man's hip, knocking him down. Jack's hand tensed into a fist and he prepared for another attack.

For a split second, the old Thandalian eyed Jack with a sober scowl, then took up his persona again. "This Vandal kicked me!" he shouted. "Vandal just kicked an old man. For no reason!" A crowd quickly formed, seeing the helpless man sprawled and the strong young Vandal—a human of Earth, in this case—looming over him, fist cocked.

A young elven-eared man stepped forward from the crowd, sword half-out and flanked by several others. "Vandal scum, what are you doing here?"

So-addan raised her hands and tried to explain, but she wasn't in her official robes and looked like any other teenage Thandalian. "No, no. Please, step back! We're with the princess."

"*We're* with the princess," the young fighter said, disregarding her and looking at Jack, "and you're like Ghistalli, who covers his ears like a Vandal and steals and kills. We just got rid of him, and now you show up." Several more men emerged from the crowd. They were dressed in common clothes, but Jack recognized trained fighters when he saw them. There were around eight of them, woven in among the ordinary people of the city. The leader drew his sword. "Our courts may well be overrun, but justice must be done."

Jack stepped forward, in front of So-addan, and slowly drew

his sword. "I am no friend of Ghistalli. I am from Vandalia, but I serve the princess and am training under Sage Wheeler."

A woman in the crowd called out, "That's what the monster who killed my son said. It's how they're trained to lie! All Vandals are liars."

Jack shook his head. This was too well prepared. He knew his words would do little here. "Run fast," he whispered to So-addan. "But do *not* lead them to her." She began to object, but he shouted, "Now!" and shoved her away, just as the first three fighters rushed him.

His blade raised, Jack blocked the overhead hack of the leader, then spun to block the second sword thrust. Leaping aside, he dodged the third while the next several attackers came on. Now his training told. In battle mode, he calculated his chances and quickly made a sudden rush for one of only two possible routes of escape. This route closed quickly, just as he had hoped, so he juked a wild-swinging swordsman and darted hard for the second opening.

Jack squeezed through the gap, a sword slice catching his foot as he went, parting the leather of his Jordans and cutting his heel. He ran on, ignoring the pain, as the fighters followed after him with shouts.

"Stop the Vandal!"

"He's plotting to kill the princess!"

These accusations followed him, occasionally causing him to have to dive aside as an angry citizen lunged for him. Jack was fleet of foot and quick of mind, and he was comfortable running away. But he didn't know where he was going, so he looked for clues to inform his escape.

At last, he saw something hopeful.

Quarry in the Quarry

Jack dashed across a bridge that spanned a short gorge leading to a stone quarry. Looking up, he saw a series of pulleys above huge stones being cut and carried away. There were chains and ropes all over, dangling down from high cranes, while the ground was littered with stout carts pulled by strong beasts. Jack sped up, rushing to the end of the bridge. A backward glance showed his pursuers had reached the bridge and were racing after him. He ran into the quarry and darted along the edge of several rock piles. The quarry was large, with workers cutting, carting, or guiding the hoisted stones. A huge uncut stone the size of a school bus stood in the center of the operation. Men on its edges were slowly cutting through the stone with intense effort and concentration.

"Stop the Vandal!" came the angry shouts behind Jack. "He's conspiring to kill the princess! Stop him!"

Jack glanced back and saw them nearing as he tired. When he turned forward again, an enormous arm shot out and clotheslined him. He got his hands up in time to soften the blow on his neck, but it still sent him sprawling. The large hands of the quarryman grasped for Jack, but he quickly kicked at his attacker's teeth, driving him back. The swordsmen were nearly on him, so he sprang up, bringing with him a handful of dirt.

The leader raised his sword and sprang. Jack waited a beat, then flung his handful of dirt at the eyes of the foremost attacker. The sword slice missed. The attackers in back rammed into their cursing companions ahead.

Jack narrowly dodged a bludgeoning punch from the bloody-mouthed quarryman, then dashed up the nearest pile of rocks, recovering his feet and balancing deftly as some gave way. He leaped for a swinging chain and rode its momentum away, then reached for a rope, swinging along till he climbed up and dropped onto the top of the rock pile, some twenty feet high.

The band of attackers came on, climbing up the rock pile and struggling as the rocks gave way. Jack balanced at the top and had a good vantage point for kicking out and slicing down at his attackers. But they outnumbered and surrounded him.

And one had a rifle.

The rifleman aimed at Jack. A shot rang out, its booming report echoing against the stone.

Jack Zulu fell.

Chapter Eighteen

Condemnation and Consequences

Jack crashed down the backside of the rock pile, curling into a protective tuck as he rolled.

Pain screamed as he settled on the bottom. *Was I shot?*

He leaned on an elbow and prepared to rise, but heard more shouts and shots and pulled his knees up and tucked his head down between his arms. When the shooting stopped, he looked up.

Steve looked down at him with a mixture of anger and concern. "You hit, kid?"

Jack looked himself over, feeling for the most painful places. They appeared to merely be bruises from his fall. "I don't think so."

"What has happened?" Wheeler asked, stepping forward, the prism blade out.

Jack rose, with Wheeler's hand to help him. "They jumped us. Is So-addan okay?"

"She's fine, back at the apartment," Steve said. "Where we should be."

'Wheeler gazed around, wary. "Let us go now."

"The rifle?" Jack asked, squinting as he looked around and began to limp after the two older men. "Did he miss me?"

"He did not get his shot off," Wheeler said, nodding at Steve.

Steve reloaded his revolver as they walked, eyes darting around the quarry. Soon more soldiers arrived, Captain Bon-hadden's swooping skite emblem on their shoulders.

Wheeler thanked them as they formed up around the three human visitors, while some tended to the mess left in the quarry.

In half an hour, after some misdirection in the streets, they were back at the apartment. Along the way, Jack had explained what Banda told them. Steve hurried to check on Michelle, and Wheeler lingered by Jack and Benny's room. Wheeler looked inside the room. "Where is Benny?"

"He and Tytrus were going to meet back up and come back together."

Wheeler frowned. "They separated? Benny is on his own?"

Jack nodded. "I'm sorry, Wheeler. I came here to help Michelle and the cause, but I'm not living up to the responsibility. I froze in the fight at the Ruins of Balmard and now I let Benny wander off and I put So-addan in danger. I feel like I'm letting everyone down. It's all going so bad."

"Come now, son." Wheeler placed a gentle hand on Jack's neck. "Despair is Satan's certainty. But we do not know all, so we cannot give in to despair."

"I feel guilty."

Wheeler coughed. "That an organized band of Becker Ghistalli's Vandal agents in the city surprised you? That you managed to get So-addan safely away while you bravely drew them to yourself and fought them off till help came from your friends?"

"I split from Tytrus and Benny because I was frustrated with them."

"Why?"

"Because I wanted to get back to Michelle."

"Ah, to get back to your duty," Wheeler said.

"Yeah," Jack agreed, "but it's more than duty. There's selfishness in it too. Pride and jealousy and anger and worry and . . ." he trailed off.

Wheeler smiled. "Those things are sometimes there in the mix of emotions and intentions to be sure. But you were doing the right thing. You must see that. You cannot have a perfect heart in this world, but you can let virtue master the wicked intentions that creep up and call out. That is as much a discipline as a desire. Discipline shapes desire."

"Wheeler, I feel like a failure. Like I've been one and I'm gonna be one. And not on a baseball team or a school assignment. No, like, when the world is in the balance and Michelle needs me."

Wheeler took Jack's shoulders in his hands. "Listen to me now, Jack. Do you know what Satan's name is?"

"The devil?"

"Aye, the devil. *Diabolos*. Do you know what that word means?"

"Evil?"

"Aye, but why evil? The name means to throw stones—to *accuse*. He is the Accuser. Do not, my dear boy, do the enemy's job for him."

"But what if I *am* guilty?"

153

"We are all of us guilty," Wheeler said, smiling wide, "but the enemy wants that to be the end of the story. It is not. The story is not over. Forgiveness is ours and a chance to start again. Again and again. We must turn not to the Accuser but to the Advocate. There—*there*—my good friend, will we find the way of life."

Jack laughed, feeling a lightness break into his heavy heart. "You're preaching, Wheeler."

Wheeler grinned and hugged Jack. "I give you the same sermon I give myself. Have a humble heart and active hands, my friend. Now, Jack, I am off to find Timman and Bonhadden. Do not despair. Be sober and think rightly, and say your prayers."

Wheeler left, and Jack did try to pray, kneeling by his bedside till he heard the door open.

"Jack, you hurt?" Benny asked.

"Not too bad," Jack replied, standing with a wince.

"I'm glad you're okay. Dude, I got into the gnarliest situation, man."

"How'd you get out?" Jack asked, worried.

"No, man," Benny answered, his hands rising in a gesture of calm, "it was so cool. I met up with this family of balloon merchants. They all make them and ride them, or whatever you call it. They took me up! I saw the whole city, man. It was amazing."

Jack's heart eased further, relieved that Benny was okay. "I saw the House of Thandal from above, the palace, this awesome lake—majorly cool. We zoomed over to the far wall and saw those very creepy mountain cliffs when the moon started to rise. Halloween-type situation. I saw the platform where

Michelle's gonna do her thing tomorrow. It's super high up, and lots of folks will be able to see her up there—like, I don't know, a hundred thousand—and it's gonna be amazing. If she does the firewings thing—and that's what everyone wants to see—then she can swoop around the whole city, and, I'm telling you, man, it will be the most epic thing."

Jack grinned, inexplicably feeling better than before. "I'm glad you're okay, B. I was worried about you. I'm sorry I left. I thought you guys weren't taking the situation with Michelle seriously."

"Dude, my bad." Benny extended a hand, and the boys did their ritual high-five and handshake combo. "I know I don't think about her the way you do, but I do care about her. I want her to win, for us to win. I was feeling useless, so I wanted to stick around and explore and see if there was anything helpful I could do. I was looking for food to cook for the team, for rations for our trip back. I found a few things, too. That's when I met the sky slider family."

"Was there a Miss Sky Slider in the family?" Jack asked, poking at Benny.

"There were a couple of daughters in the right age vector," Benny said, bowing theatrically. "I got my balloon tour from one such daughter. So, kind of a date."

"What would Vayner say?" Jack asked. Vayner was a Garthian girl who Benny had a close friendship with. They didn't get to see each other often, but they exchanged letters by way of Jack and Michelle.

"Vayner is probably out of my league, Jack," Benny replied. "I think she'd love for us to wear matching 'Just Friends' sweatshirts. I think I'm sunk on that front."

"I'm not so sure," Jack said. "But anyway, what's the Than-dalian balloonist's name?"

"Either Biscan or Bicsan," Benny said. "I was afraid to ask her to clarify. I kept calling her Biscuit."

"Smooth, man."

"Yeah, she thought it was a nickname, so I just went with it. Their family was super cool. Her brother came with us on the ride, too."

"What's his name, Gravy?"

"Alas, no. I heard him say it, but it did not stick in the old melon."

"I hope you can see them again," Jack said.

"Me, too." Benny crossed and sagged onto his bed. "I'd like for you to meet them, if we have time."

There was a knock at the door, and Tytrus poked his head in. "Conference, now."

They jumped up. Jack winced at the bruises—especially one bad one on his ribs—and followed Tytrus. Winding through the corridors, they came to a room the size of a high school classroom back home. Inside sat Bon-hadden, alongside other Thandalian officers, Timman, Steve, Wheeler, and So-addan. Thandalian rangers and more of Bon-hadden's men, all armed to the teeth, stood at attention by all three doors.

Jack hurried to So-addan and embraced her. "I'm so glad you're okay," he said.

"You too," she replied. "Thank you, Jack. I got away because of you."

"And I was saved because of you. Thank you. Are you hurt at all?"

"Not really, no. A few scrapes. They wanted to take you

156

out. They let me go."

Timman called for quiet. "This will not take long. Captain Bon-hadden has taken the lead in securing the safety of the princess. We have had our differences, but he has done well, and I honor him." With this, he gave a short bow to the heroic captain. He continued. "I am reliably informed, and the captain confirms this from his intelligence assets as well, that there will be an attack on the princess tomorrow night. We are formulating a plan to counter that, including eliminating known threats tonight and considering—I say, only considering—moving the princess tomorrow, after her speech."

Captain Bon-hadden bowed.

Wheeler nodded. "We all agree that her safety is paramount."

Timman went on. "Looking to tomorrow—to the reason we have come. I have insisted upon directing the proceedings of the speech and presentation for noon. The princess will be led to the platform from the underground hall and the interior stairs. She will be accompanied on that platform by myself, Sage Wheeler, Captain Bon-hadden, Chief Steve, and her servant, So-addan."

Jack's heart sank, and anger surged up in him. "She would want me there!" he said bitterly. "Have you asked her?"

Timman nodded. "The princess has been consulted. You," he said, looking over Jack, Benny, and Tytrus, "have been irresponsible tonight. You will not be close to the princess."

Chapter Nineteen

Ascending

Jack woke from a night of fitful sleep, still fuming. Benny was snoring from way-too-nearby, so Jack rolled quietly out of bed and got dressed in silence. But he wanted to shout.

Jack dressed quickly in his clean shirt and pants, then pulled on his freshly pressed coat. He left his damaged Jordans and slipped on his more official dress boots, ending with buckling on his sword at his left side. His revolver he wore on his right hip, and his father's badge was tucked into an inner pocket of his jacket, along with some extra ammo.

Jack cracked the door and was stepping through when he heard Benny yawn. Jack turned back to see his friend sitting up.

Benny blinked and rubbed his eyes. "What time is it?"

"It's early, B. I'm out."

"Hold on, man," Benny said, kicking his covers off and rising amid a yawn. "Where you going, dude?"

Jack looked at the wall, then the ceiling. "Just for a walk."

Benny was smiling when Jack made eye contact. "I know what you're doing."

"Oh, really? What am I doing?" Jack asked, an edge to his voice.

"Hey, easy, Jack," Benny said, stepping closer with arms outstretched. "I'm your guy, ya' know?"

Jack accepted the embrace, then, when they broke apart, shrugged. "Yeah, I'm going to see if I can get on that platform. I'm going to see if I can get closer."

Benny nodded. "Uh, huh."

"I've got to do it, B. Got to. I can't let anything happen to her."

Benny nodded again. "I'm with you, Jack. You know that. But it kinda is what it is. You're in the gallery, which isn't too far away. At least you got invited to that, man. Cause you're a hero, right? They do know that. They do respect you. They had to cut off dignitaries for the platform somewhere, and you're just behind the cut. I know you're not used to that, but—"

"It's not about making a cut, Benny!" Jack insisted. "I don't need to be in the place of honor." He paused, a small voice inside him whispering *Liar*. He went on. "It's about *her*, man. It's all about her! I can't let her get hurt."

Benny nodded yet again. "I know, bro. I know. You're right; you're right! But you also can't control the world. You're not Rancast—sorry, I shouldn't have said that. But you can't control all this stuff. She's gotta fly solo today. And you can't get carried around with her like Mr. Lois Lane with your sword out swiping at bad guys. You gotta do you, and let her do her."

"I need to be on that platform, Benny. I have to be."

"Look, man, I got no ticket at all. I am officially kicked to the curb. If I had a ticket, it would say 'Curb 1A.' I care about Michelle too. You know I do. But I can't get into the gallery.

I've got to find my own way. But the gallery, man. That's where everybody who's anybody wants to be, and you're there. That means you matter. Michelle probably had to fight like crazy to get you there. But it's done, man. It's all been arranged. That's where you're gonna be."

"It's too far away!" Jack snapped. "There will be balconies and balloons and high windows and towers, and it's too easy for Ghistalli's men to get to her. You heard Banda! They're still in the city. I can't just sit there in the gallery with the second sacred elder of Bumtown and his wife while Michelle's in danger!"

Benny pulled Jack gently down to where he was seated on his bed. "Yeah, dude. It's lousy. But you know they've accounted for all the balconies, windows, and balloons. They have people everywhere. They also have that crazy *Star Trek* shield for the platform, which is supposed to keep out pretty much everything. Wheeler shared that with us in private to ease your mind."

"Did you notice that his mind didn't seem eased?" Jack asked, his leg twitching in a nonstop bouncing motion.

Benny grimaced. "Yes, I did notice that. But it's totally natural, man. This is risky. It's all tough for all of us. We knew it was going to be risky—the whole thing—when we planned the trip. We're here. It's dangerous, yeah. But it's also time. It's showtime, Jack."

And I'm not in the show. Jack closed his eyes, fingers tenting over his nose as he inhaled deeply. "Thanks for the talk." He rose and walked to the door. Turning back, he said, "See you out there, B."

He left.

Hours later Jack was in the gallery, after failing at every above- and below-board tactic he could think of to get on the platform. The gallery was made of a smooth kind of sculpted concrete and reminded Jack of the far more modest bleachers at Myrtle High's football field. The platform on the tower top was a huge round stage, flat but for the throne that rose in its center. Surrounding the tower was the city center itself, alive and vibrant, with thousands watching from several seating platforms that were attached in rungs from the central spire to the high platform. The highest of these was the gallery Jack had been assigned to, which was nearly touching the platform and provided the best view of proceedings of anywhere in the city. Balloons filled the air, many with banners of support hanging from their baskets. The nearby mountain range cliffs loomed in the near-distance, an arresting and somber beauty that contrasted dramatically with the buoyant mood of the people of Destrow.

The platform was empty as noon approached, anticipation reaching its zenith all around. An occasional odd shimmer revealed a barely visible half-globe shield surrounding the platform. Jack had tested it upon arrival and received a painful jolt as he withdrew his hand. As the pain changed to numbness, he recognized he would not be crossing that boundary. This both frustrated and reassured him.

Jack was seated next to a young elder from a nearby village. In fact, it was the village that Consul Timman hailed from. Jack enjoyed their conversation as the big moment neared and was quietly grateful for the distraction. Each of the few outworld dignitaries in the gallery was given an earpiece that would, he was told, translate the Thandalian language of the speakers. Jack knew that even Michelle, who had painstakingly studied, would be speaking in that tongue.

Gazing around, Jack searched for Benny and Tytrus, but he could not locate them below in the sea of exuberant Thandalians in colorful clothing.

Jack gazed at the stage, then down at the long tower. At any moment, perhaps now, Michelle was traveling up that spire in some kind of elvish elevator and would eventually reach the spiral stairway, ascending to emerge onto the platform. He had been thinking of himself so much, but a pang of worry for her own task hit him.

Michelle was expected to fly. To give a rousing speech that would go down in history and then burst into the purple sky. Jack assumed someone was ready with the shield—to deactivate it—once she took flight. He rose quickly, pacing and glowering at the platform. *Where's the switch? Who's in charge of it? Can they be trusted?* A hundred new worries worked through his mind, his heart beating fast as he shook his head and ground his teeth.

"Are you well, young master?" the young elder asked. "You seem agitated."

Jack blinked, then nodded. "I guess I am agitated. I . . . I, uh, I just want this to go well."

"As do we all, Jack," the elder replied, motioning for him to sit again beside him. "But you block the view for others with your pacing, and I believe the moment has come."

Jack sat with a shrug and focused on the stage. And they

came then, to the raucous applause of the watching city. Consul Timman emerged first from a hatch in the ground, beneath which lay a white staircase. Jack was surprised to see that he wore the regalia of a sage, with the medallion around his neck last seen by Jack on the Thandalian sage who had awarded him his own medal at the Wayfarer's Inn. Then Captain Bon-hadden came, spectacular in full military dress, alongside Steve, who wore a striking suit that featured a long black jacket. Bon-hadden and Steve flanked the opening of the stairwell, while Timman strode to the center of the stage.

Jack fidgeted. *I guess Wheeler is with Michelle.*

Timman motioned for silence, raising his arms. "*Than-dullo han flinco...*" he began, and Jack heard this over the amplification, but in his ear came the almost-simultaneous translation. "My countrymen. I am honored to be here as one of your own." The crowd cheered loud and long, so that he had to raise his hands again for quiet. "But today is not about me, though today I take up the mantle that I have long prepared for. Our own sage of the last six years, Orpellian the Wise, has died." A gasp went up from the crowd, and Jack felt his heart sink. The venerable sage had been old and ill, so it wasn't a great surprise. Everyone knew that Timman would be sage in her place. Timman went on. "We will mourn her and do the proper rites in time. I am sage-in-waiting only and will do my best to serve until those rituals are done to honor her life and finalize my appointment. But today is not about the fall or rise of sages. It is about higher things. Sages are of the soil, but Thaons ascend to the skies!" He raised his hands, exultant, and the city exploded in cheers. Louder, he continued. "I saw the last Thaon fly over the Wayland! I watched her rout the crows of Kaalgrad in her spectacular brightness. I saw it all, and it was glorious!"

Timman closed his eyes and bowed his head, pausing as the crowd quieted down to silence. "I also knew her as my student. As one who learned at my feet. Imagine that, a virtual god receiving instruction from a child of the Destronn Plain."

Steve's eyes narrowed as he gazed around at the roaring crowd. Bon-hadden seemed to sink a moment, and Steve's arm twitched as if to help him. But the old captain straightened, nodded to Steve, and resumed his own inspection of the surrounding crowds. Jack exhaled. *What's wrong with me? I'm looking for trouble. This is a day to celebrate.* He tried to talk himself into a more optimistic mood, but his worries persisted.

Timman waited for the latest applause to fade, then continued. "This is a day we have long awaited. The rising of a new vision of victory, a new leader to take us into our true destiny." He turned toward the stairwell and extended his open hands in welcome. "Bring the princess out."

There was silence then, as Michelle emerged from the stairwell top, clad in a white robe with a golden pattern of astonishing brightness and beauty. Her hair spilled out behind her, revealing elven ears beneath a spectacular crown of gold. Poised and regal, she crossed the distance slowly. So-addan came in her train, head down and holding Michelle's flowing golden cape. So-addan herself wore only a white gown, but her hair was braided and beautiful, and happy tears were in her eyes.

Michelle's eyes were clear. Her head erect, she seemed neither proud nor common but certain of her place and her role in this moment. Jack's heart swelled, and he longed to be near her. He felt happy, hopeful, and grateful, but beneath those feelings lay a dread. He immediately attributed it to selfishness. *The greater she becomes, the farther she gets from me. Unless I...* Jack shook the thought away.

Timman welcomed Michelle with a brief bow and a kiss on both cheeks. Jack couldn't see Michelle's face now, and he looked around to see if it was possible to improve his angle. It wasn't, not without making a scene. Everyone in the gallery sat riveted. Timman raised a hand. "It is time, oh Thaon of Andos, for you to fulfill your destiny."

A guttural boom sounded, and everyone looked up to the source of the sound. It had come from the cliffs. A near building's balcony exploded in a spray of bricks, orange-red fire belching out black billowing smoke as broken bodies fell from the heights.

Screams. More blasts far off, growing nearer. People scrambling from the gallery. Fear. Anger. Shock. More screams.

Jack looked back up at the cliffs and saw shapes rising into the sky, quickly flying toward them. More thumping booms followed, and shattering blasts blew apart the defensive turrets along the wall.

Jack swiveled back to gaze at the tower top and saw a confused flurry of action there. He glanced sideways and, seeing a blur of steel, tried to sidestep as a knife drove into his back.

Sudden, striking pain hit him, but he had no time to process it. He was dodging the second blow and squaring up on his attacker. It was the young Thandalian elder, casting aside his knife and drawing a blaster. Jack kicked out and missed the weapon, then spun, ripping free his blade and striking the man down as he fired just over Jack's head.

Jack turned again, his back bleeding as he reached to feel for his wound, and peered through the smoke and chaos to the tower platform.

The hazy shield remained, but through it Jack saw Timman grab at Michelle and draw a blaster. Steve drew but held his fire as Timman hooked his arm around Michelle's neck and pulled her in front of him. Bon-hadden reached for his blade, but before he could draw it Timman shot and killed him. Timman then turned his weapon on Steve.

Jack screamed out "No!" and ran for the platform as Timman fired twice again. Steve jerked, reeled back, then fell limply into the staircase hatch.

Chapter Twenty

Slow Hands
and a Proud Heart

S teve was gone. Wheeler was nowhere to be seen. Jack was alone in the chaotic gallery, and he couldn't get to Michelle.

Glancing up, he saw the sky was filled with enemies. Shard-harks—those lethal mothmen of living nightmares—swept over the city, dropping firebombs from their bandoliers and slicing down escaping Thandalians. Vandal militia—either human-like or red-headbanded traitor Thandalians hiding their ears—flew in on various kinds of hang gliders and other inventive vehicles. They laughed as they fired rifles into the crowd of noncombatants. Another kind of flyer, small paracopters with stunning agility, was employed by others. These zipped around launching rockets and spraying fire across the sky, burning civilians' balloons so that innocent Thandalians plunged to fiery deaths.

The Rancastian banner, an upside-down star in a circle with a three-pronged crown above it, was borne by the invaders. Everywhere this emblem appeared, on the gliders and copters and from flags flown by the bloodthirsty fighters filling the city, death and destruction followed.

Jack was desperate to help. But he didn't know what to do or where to turn. The gallery was hit by another blast, and the back part of it tore off and fell in pieces to the crowd far below. Some terrified men and women, moments ago eagerly watching the triumphant celebration of the Last Thaon in their city, were now clinging to the edge of a crumbling gallery. Jack wanted to help them, but his attention was on Michelle. Timman had her by the neck, a gun pointed at her head. Jack was trapped outside the shield, his head darting back and forth. *Where is Wheeler?*

All around the tower platform, bombs and gunfire battered the city. The shield held, which was good, but Timman was inside the shield, and he had Michelle. Jack watched as some distant glancing shots seemed to bounce off the mostly invisible barrier. A paracopter piloted by a Vandal attacker veered overhead, firing down on him. Jack dove for cover under the first row of concrete benches, wincing against the spray of shattered cement. Through the thin slits of his vision he saw that the close-range gunfire seemed to temporarily break open a small section of the shield wall.

When the paracopter zoomed past, blasting away at another target now, Jack sprang up. He drew his revolver and fired one shot at the shield. It crackled and seemed to create an opening about the size of his head. He ran up and stuck his arm through it. It closed quickly, and he drew it out just in time.

Inside, Michelle struggled to break free. She was being dragged across the platform by Timman, who, as she resisted, struck her repeatedly in the head with his gun.

Looking away with rage and glancing around at the scene of chaos and carnage, Jack took a few leaping steps back, then squared up to the platform. Aiming his revolver at one area, he shot and ran ahead, firing all five remaining rounds as the circle of broken shield grew wider. Reaching the edge, he dove through.

Jack landed inside as the crackling shield wall closed behind him, rolling into a crouch. He holstered his empty gun and gazed ahead. So-addan was weeping, pleading with her father to let Michelle go. Michelle was choking, straining at the strangling arm Timman had cinched around her neck. Another blow fell from Timman's gun hand, and blood trickled down from Michelle's temple. Jack leapt into a run, quietly crossing the distance in seconds. Timman saw him then, and turning, he slung Michelle down and brought his weapon up to fire at Jack. But Jack was too close now, and his deftly drawn blade arced out and found Timman's outstretched gun hand, slicing it off. Jack didn't stop but stepped close and drove the blade at the betrayer's heart.

Timman was quick, and he sidestepped the stab and drew his own blade in one swift motion. Ignoring his bloody stump, Timman attacked. Jack was quickly defending himself against a surprisingly energetic assault from the man who was now wounded and one-handed. It didn't seem to slow him down. Timman was, to Jack's surprise, an incredible swordsman. It took all of Jack's concentration to escape an immediate death.

Jack blocked an overhead slice, then felt Timman's boot in his chest, knocking him flat and breathless. Jack rolled over and coughed as Timman came on. A kick in the face sent Jack sprawling, and Timman loomed over him, poised for a final strike. But So-addan stepped between them, her hands up and voice pleading, giving Jack enough time to recover and regain his feet.

"Out of the way!" Timman shouted, angrily sidestepping his daughter as he rejoined the fight. Jack met him, grateful for the pause in the frightening contest. He glanced over at Michelle. Her hand was at her bleeding temple, and she was struggling to get to her knees. A surge of fury filled him. He didn't wait for Timman's attack; Jack ran at the traitor. Timman blocked Jack's fierce assault, moving skillfully and absorbing the worst. But Jack's power showed, with two-handed overhead strikes mixed in with stabbing thrusts and whirlwind slices, causing Timman to retreat slowly to the edge of the platform.

A fire raged inside Jack, a feeling of well-being that surged up from within, into and through his limbs. He went from a wild fury to an almost serene ecstasy in his attack, his concentrating eye anticipating Timman's every artful advance. He blocked and spun, kicked and sliced, a virtual dance of sword craft that Timman only survived by astonishing skill and energy.

Jack felt invincible then, imagining the eyes of an admiring crowd upon him. It seemed his power was limitless, his intelligence unmatched, and his skills imperious. His blood was golden, flowing from the heart of a creature unlike anything the worlds had ever seen. He seemed to glide ahead, attacking with an odd ease, deft as the cleverest master but strong as a colossal monster. Jack remembered Timman firing and Steve pitching over and then the sight of him spilling Michelle's blood. And the rage came again.

"You liar!" Jack cried, pounding Timman down with blow after blow of his blade. "You murdering coward!"

Timman crumbled, bent down and blocking with the last of his failing strength. "Jack!" he cried. "Stop, Jack!"

But Jack would not stop. In his frenzy he hammered down, and the hated face of this betraying Thandalian became every Thandalian's face, beaten down and defeated and ready to die. He hammered on, feeling a surge of pride and power unmatched in his history—perhaps in all of history. Jack blinked, and he saw Timman, grim and defiant. Then he blinked again and saw Tytrus, So-addan, the refugee boy, Dunny, and the thousand other Thandalians he had known. The quavering blade he hammered down on showed the reflection of a huge figure, beautiful and brilliant, the ruler of all worlds.

The sword's reflection showed Rancast.

Jack gasped and stepped back, stunned and blinking. There was a moment, then, when he knew he could end Timman's life—end his threat. He knew he should do it, but the sick trick of feeling like he had become Rancast spoiled the duty. So he hesitated. He hesitated only a moment.

And then it was too late.

Chapter Twenty-One

Pride
and Blood

J ack stepped ahead again, his moment of hesitation over and his blade raised high. But just then an explosion rocked the tower, and he was knocked off his feet. Scrambling to his knees, he saw the shield wall fall and three enemy paracopters fly in, with flanking shardharks swooping down. The shardharks glided down to stand, war hammers out, between Jack and Timman.

Rancast's star-crown banner was planted on the tower top. A grizzled figure with a red band around his head—over the tops of his ears—stepped out of one of the larger paracopters. Jack recognized him from images he had seen in the Wayland.

Becker Ghistalli. Rancast's ruling warlord in Thandalia.

The returning rebel leader looked around contemptuously. He smiled at Michelle, who had just regained her feet, hands feeling at her injured neck. So-addan knelt weeping nearby. Bon-hadden's body lay still, and Ghistalli laughed at the sight. "I beat you again, old fool," he rasped. Then his gaze fixed on Jack. "You are Lord Rancast's particular favorite. He turned to Timman here only after you did not accept his first invitation.

So I will again invite you, young Jack. Come to him, as we all have, and with us rule the worlds."

Jack shook his head, regret and longing insistent inside him. "No thanks, you psycho."

Ghistalli smiled, then stepped forward and, swifter than Jack imagined possible, kicked Jack in the chest. Jack felt a crunch of bones and was sent rapidly backwards to slide along the surface of the platform. His ribs ached, and he struggled to inhale. He seemed to be trying to breathe through a thin straw and coughed and gagged in agony. He was near the hatch now and thought of crawling over and collapsing into it. He wasn't sure he could. Twisting back, his ribs complained and he was certain something wasn't right with them. His back radiated pain from the knife wound, and his head was spinning.

A medic from Ghistalli's staff was wrapping Timman's bloody stump and securing that arm in a sling. Ghistalli barked orders through a kind of walkie-talkie, and several of his men returned to their paracopters. A few flew off. Jack assumed they went to help lead the recapture of the city.

It had all been a trap, of course. Jack could see that, now. Ghistalli hadn't really lost the city; he only withdrew to the surrounding cliffs to lure the Thandalians into pouring into an arena where he could decimate the loyalist army and their civilian counterparts. It was wickedly genius, and Jack saw Rancast's legendary intellect at work. Timman was a key piece, and Rancast had played him perfectly.

Jack clutched at his chest, feeling beneath his shirt the small pawn on its chain, and dragged in ragged breaths. He wondered if he would ever breathe freely again. *Where is Wheeler? They must have killed or captured him already—before this.* Jack tried to get to his knees but slumped back down in the struggle, his ribs and back screaming in pain.

Ghistalli called out his last orders, then turned to Timman. "Our lord is pleased, of course. You have kept your promise. He will keep his and allow you your journey."

"With her?" Timman asked, nodding at Michelle. "As he promised?"

"Yes," Ghistalli answered in a guttural growl. "She is your key to the Golden City. But do not forget that she is also key to our master's plans. She will join him as one of his worldbrides. So do not let her come to any serious harm."

"Of course not. I never intended to harm her."

"You have so far passed the test, Timman," Ghistalli said, "but a final trial remains. The oath is made in blood and sacrifice. As you know. As you were warned. As is fitting for all good fortune. As it was with me, it shall also be with you, by our lord's unerring command."

Timman grimaced a moment; then his face grew calm and he nodded. "I recall the oath."

Ghistalli scowled and gazed up at the sky. "When I was given charge of Lord Rancast's armies in this realm, I was asked to show I was loyal by a hard choice—a choice that made going back to who I had been impossible. It is his will that you do the same." He nodded across toward Michelle.

So-addan, Timman's only daughter, had placed herself between them and the princess. Wheezing, Jack tried to get to his feet, but he could barely breathe, and he collapsed again. Through tears in his eyes, he watched Timman stride forward, his good hand flexing as he walked.

So-addan's face was twisted in grief. "Daddy? Daddy, please. Leave her alone. Don't take her. Don't do this! Daddy, no!"

Timman's face flinched, his eye twitched, then his expression hardened into resolve. He drew his sword. Jack looked away as the final scream sounded and the atrocious blow fell.

When Jack looked back, So-addan's body lay motionless on the platform, and Timman had Michelle—shocked into horrified silence—in his grasp once again.

Becker Ghistalli nodded, a sick smile playing over his hardened face. "Welcome to the Lord's Council, Timman."

Timman said nothing, only jerked Michelle along and, with the help of several of Ghistalli's henchmen, shoved her into a paracopter. They took off.

Michelle was gone. Captured.

So-addan was gone. Dead.

Shocked and heartsore, Jack was finally able to stand. He gripped his sword, the one he should have used to kill Timman moments before, and raised it. He staggered forward, certain this was his end.

Ghistalli saw him and smiled. "Joining us at last?" he growled. "You are a Vandal already, after all. And there is a place on the council for you, young Jack. You may rule a realm, like the rest of the few and great, when he has conquered all. Vandalia itself may be yours, which would be a high honor indeed. Think of it, boy. You could be ruler of all your world. He can give that to you. Just follow him. Follow him now into the power and the glory."

Jack spat, coughing and holding his ribs, then spoke through clenched teeth. "The kind of glory that comes from killing a defenseless girl? That comes from attacking unarmed civilians in the streets and in their homes? Murdering children and women and taking girls?"

Ghistalli shook his head. "There are no innocents of their kind. Do not be deceived by their lies. This is the revenge they all deserve. This is an uprising against the old oppressors—a revolution. We are the prophets of peace, and I am the hand of justice."

"Peace?" Jack gasped, motioning around at the battered, burning city and the cries of pain amid the chaos. "You are a liar, Becker Ghistalli."

Ghistalli's face bent in haughty disappointment. "Want the truth, boy? Your father died after abandoning those he swore to protect. He died when he seized the fruit of Andos for himself and tried to take the world as its master. Rancast rescued many while your father, a prideful, power-hungry monster, killed the Thaons of the Golden City and reduced it to gray ruins. I was there. I saw it all."

"Liar!" Jack screamed with ragged breath. He raised his sword and tripped ahead, rage fueling his agonizing steps.

Ghistalli's eyes narrowed, a look of contempt on his face. Nodding to a flanking gunman, he said, "Kill him," and turned to enter his paracopter. Ghistalli took off as the gunman grinned and aimed at Jack. Jack closed his eyes and thought of his mother.

Gunshots rang out.

Chapter Twenty-Two

The Fall
of Thandalia

Jack winced.

But he felt no new wounds. Opening his eyes, he saw the gunman down and the others scattering as they fired above Jack. Jack swiveled to see a paracopter glide in overheard. In the pilot's position sat Banda, hand unrelenting on the trigger, as the remaining Vandal bandits dove for cover.

Banda's stolen paracopter had been damaged badly in the battle so far. It hung at an awkward angle and, after more strikes from swooping enemies, spiraled into a fiery crash on the platform. The tower top was ablaze, and gunfire rained down from enemy paracopters, with occasional concussive blasts rocking the shaky platform.

The tower tilted dramatically, and those near the edge slid off, grasping desperately for handholds. Jack steadied himself, balancing against the shifting ground. In this new angle, he noticed something in the tilting hatchway.

Steve's hands gripped the white railing of the spiral stairway. With a groan, he pulled himself out and crawled out onto the platform. On his knees, he looked up and around, searching the chaotic stage that had so recently held his daughter.

Rebel soldiers, red headbands covering their ears, rose uneasily and leveled their guns. Jack tensed, glancing from Steve back to the attackers. The gunmen grinned.

A sudden flash of color appeared as a balloon swept up like a sunrise at the tower's edge. Pitching forward, the basket smashed into the rebels and sent them sprawling.

The balloon dipped wide in a bending arc, then rushed back in a counter swing toward Jack.

Jack saw who was in the basket. "Benny!"

"Get in!" Benny cried, leaning out and extending his arm.

Jack sheathed his blade and dipped to scoop up Steve. In a painful heave, he and Benny, along with help from a Thandalian boy Jack didn't know, got Steve into the basket. They hauled Jack in too just as more gunfire came their way and the balloon, racing on, dipped below the edge of the other side of the crumbling tower.

Jack was suddenly unbalanced at the sickening dip, and he fell to the bottom of the basket. It reminded him of a boat, but with a kind of woven wood like bamboo. Wincing, he saw that two others rode along, with one young female Thandalian piloting. They looked like siblings. The pilot played at a kind of wheel and pulled at several ropes around the controls as they swept right and left. The balloon above them was damaged but holding.

Jack crawled over to check on Steve, who lay motionless with his eyes closed.

"Is he okay?" Benny asked, his face sweaty and marked by a long red slice along his jaw.

"He's got a pulse. But he was shot." Jack found one wound near his collarbone, and he pressed it and called for any kind of bandage.

The Thandalian boy knelt and tore off his shirt, then stepped in to press on the wound. Jack collapsed back as the basket swung again and held on tight.

"*Tindro-hock loma honan!*" the pilot cried, eyes wild as she pointed back.

Jack stood painfully and gaped back at the tower as it broke apart and collapsed down into the churning streets below.

The piloted balloon swung through the chaos above the city, dipping low under the fire of paracopters and sweeping up again as the explosions rocked the buildings beside and below them. Jack gazed, mouth agape.

Fire. Fire everywhere. Explosions every few seconds. Gunshots continuous. Balloons to their left and right raced to escape, all around they were being shot down to fall in fiery crashes.

And screams. Screams of pain and horror and shock and broken hearts.

This was supposed to be a day of triumph, the day that would begin the winning of the war. But the reverse had happened. The trap laid was sprung, and the Thandalian cause was caught. Caught and crushed.

"Michelle," Jack said—to no one—his voice quavering. He gazed down at the city and, eyes wide with shock, whispered his lament. "I lost Michelle, to the traitor Timman. I watched her go. I lost her. I could have—"

Benny drew near. "Okay, Jack. We lost her. But right now we've got to focus on getting out of here, buddy."

Jack blinked, and nodded. "What now?"

The Thandalian boy spoke up. "We make for the Destronn Hollow. The loyalist forces will regroup there, I'm certain."

Benny nodded. "It's not that far away, Jack. I think we can make it."

Jack looked down and saw that Steve's wound had received an excellent field dressing, improvised with the young man's shirt and some rope. "Thank you."

"The second shot was a graze only," he replied. "So this is the one to watch. I'll take care of him until we can make it to the rendezvous."

Steve blinked, inhaled deeply, and then looked around, shocked. He tried to stand. "Where is she?" he growled, coughing.

Benny knelt and put his hands on Steve's shoulders. "Chief Robinson, it's okay. We're trying to escape. Just sit still."

"Still!" Steve cried, tossing Benny aside and rising. "Where is she, Jack?"

"Gone," Jack said. "I lost her."

Steve's face twisted in a grimace of agony. "No. *No!*"

The balloon dipped quickly, then rose, racing over a high building, before sweeping sideways as a paracopter zipped into view on the right. It opened fire, and they ducked into the basket. But the bullets mostly missed as they dipped again, placing a towering turret between them and the paracopter.

With the balloon very low now, they could see a clash in the streets below. Ghistalli's rebels attacked civilians in the square while loyalist soldiers tried desperately to protect them. Jack, remembering his spare bullets, carefully reloaded his revolver. As they sped past, he fired into the enemy attackers, shouting as he squeezed the trigger again and again.

A masked Vandal with a rocket launcher on his shoulder turned and aimed at them. The rocket ripped through the air and exploded near their balloon, sending it careening off course to collide with a paracopter and its surprised pilot. Tangled up a moment, the balloon plunged as the paracopter swerved and dove. The balloon unhitched at last, and their pilot screamed. The Thandalian boy leapt to help her. The paracopter swept around and prepared to fire.

Steve stood and quickly drew his gun. Closing one eye, he fired one shot that killed the pilot and sent the paracopter diving to its doom. It crashed and blew up amid the rebel force.

Steve sagged and holstered his gun.

Jack bent to help him, but the Thandalian boy knelt and tended to Steve. The pilot pulled on her rope controls, and this sent the balloon higher, rising on the warm winds over Destrow.

Benny pointed ahead and down. They were nearly over the gate they had entered a day before. In a nauseating contrast to their ecstatic entrance, the crowd below was pouring out of the city in a horrified panic. Women. Children. The elderly and infirm. Many men defended their retreat with what weapons they had, falling in scores, as others joined the mass of people fleeing in terror.

Gunfire ripped through the balloon, fraying it further and causing them to drop. There were loud explosions all around. A burst of flack hit just beside them, and the pilot screamed again as the basket tore and fire caught on its edge.

They plunged, still staggering ahead in wild spurts, but their flight had become a fall—and a fiery one, too. The flames spread up and over the balloon. The Thandalian siblings fought with the controls, even as their rope levers burned beside them.

Dropping faster than they progressed forward, the balloon barely made it over the gate, scraping its basket on the crumbling parapets. Jack nearly pitched over and out, but Benny's hand shot out and gripped him tight. His best friend was anchored in a corner nook below black smoke and tattered nylon that flapped like a battered old flag.

They flew along, a wounded bird on fire, just above the scattering masses of fallen Destrow. Ghistalli's forces fired on them, from hills and the road and flying machines. Shardharks darted down to kill, then up and down, again and again. Jack aimed his gun but couldn't be sure he would hit what he meant to. *So many children and mothers!* Gritting his teeth, he holstered his weapon and held on as they fell lower and lower.

Ahead, three shardharks landed and looked eagerly around for fresh prey. As the balloon dipped lower, the pilot cried out, "Brace!" Then she gripped the two remaining cords and ripped them back with all her might. One broke clean in her hand as they dropped suddenly, smashing into the shardharks and crashing in a fiery tumble.

Chaos in chaos. A blazing somersaulting wreck. Everywhere noise and a smell of burning.

Jack stumbled out of the ruined balloon, now a burning tangle of broken parts, and looked around. A scene of unbelievable chaos, different than peering down from high above, was revealed. Now among the furious flight of the refugees and the diabolical pursuit of the Vandal rebels, he gazed around in horror. He shook his head, only then remembering his friends. He plunged back into the ruined balloon and helped pull out Benny, as well as the injured pilot. Her arm was broken and she sobbed quietly as her brother, himself now gashed badly on his head, helped her out. Soon, they were all out.

They had all lived, though none came through unhurt.

Steve's eyes were wide as he gazed around, gun out. Almost all those around them were Thandalians, fleeing as best they could and caring for their most vulnerable as they went.

"There!" Benny called. Jack followed his pointing finger to a yellow barn. The yellow barn where they had left their horses the day before.

"Come on!" Steve said, and they all followed him. It was ten minutes in the wrong direction, against the flowing current of desperate refugees. But they pressed on and soon rushed to the barn door. Steve kicked it down, and they ran in.

They saw nothing. Heard no animal sounds, only the insistent noise of the terrified tumult outside.

Jack's heart sank.

They split up, looking over every corner. Soon Benny emerged from the back yard, bringing in two horses by their reins. Jack smiled to see Captain Kirk and rushed over to stroke the beloved mustang. The other horse was a six-legged Waylander, and Steve quickly found a saddle. The younger Thandalian sibling did the same, and Jack helped him saddle up Captain Kirk. Steve continued his work, snagging blankets and other nearby provisions and securing them on the horses.

The Thandalian boy drew near, helping his sister along. "It's southwest to Destronn Hollow—to the rendezvous."

"How is she?" Jack asked.

The sister smiled. "I'm okay."

"Thanks for getting us out of there," Jack said.

She smiled for acknowledgment, then sat heavily on a stone bench, gingerly stabilizing her bad arm with her good one.

Benny patted the large horse. "The rendezvous, yeah. We can pile a few on this guy, then a couple on Captain Kirk here. We can make it to the regroup. If they're not far away, maybe we can get out of this alive."

Steve raised a hand for silence. "Where're they taking Michelle?"

Jack inhaled deeply. "Andos."

Steve stabbed a foot in the stirrup and vaulted up, wincing as he landed and grabbing at his wound. Teeth gritted, he said, "I'm sorry. You are going to have to get to the rendezvous on foot. I'm going to Andos."

Jack nodded. "I'm coming with you."

"Then come on," Steve said.

Jack mounted his horse, and the sound of explosions, gunfire, and screams seemed to intensify outside.

Destrow had fallen. The Thandalian cause was crushed. Thandalia itself was certainly lost.

It was the end of the world.

Chapter Twenty-Three

West Virginians in the Woods

Jack and Steve persuaded Benny to go with his Thandalian friends to the rendezvous. Steve insisted it was the safest route.

"I have been to Andos before, Benny," Steve said, "and I'm positive it's better for you to join up with what's left of the resistance. Our road is more deadly than you can imagine."

"I can imagine quite a bit," Benny murmured, no smile touching his lips.

"It's worse. It's impossible. And with three, it would be harder. I can't make this harder. Find the loyalists. They'll hold out and regroup at Destronn Hollow. But you have to hurry. We only have two horses, and we can't be slowed down. We have to try to get Michelle. Help them," Steve motioned to the balloonist siblings, "and try to find any of our friends you can. Get safe, then try to get to Gate City. It'll be the last place to fall. Get home, Benny, if you can."

Benny nodded, tears in his eyes. His voice was thick with emotion. "I'd only slow you down."

"I'm sorry, kid," Steve said, snapping the reins as the horse's head came up and he began to trot away toward the wide door he had earlier kicked down. "Come on, Jack."

"Benny," Jack managed, his head swiveling from Steve ahead to Benny below him. "You're my best friend, B. Tell Mom..." he trailed off.

"I will," Benny replied, waving awkwardly as Jack urged his horse ahead, catching up to Steve.

Jack didn't look back, but he felt his stomach drop. *Will I ever see Benny again?*

Steve's eyes narrowed as he looked out from the barnyard to the chaos all around. "It's time for hard thoughts, Jack. Save the soft ones for after we get where we're going."

"Yes, sir," Jack replied, wiping at his eyes. "I'm ready to do what we have to do."

"You loaded up?"

Jack drew his revolver and checked the chamber, reloading it quickly. "Yes, sir."

"I know it's tough, but we ride hard through the chaos. It's only Michelle—only Michelle now, in all the world. In all the worlds. We can't fix all this," he motioned to the scene of fleeing refugees pursued by murderous rebels, "but we might be able to help her. And helping her helps all of them."

Jack nodded. "We'll have to come close to the city gate to get on the road to Andos. Won't that be the way they're taking her?"

"They'll take that road, by air as far as they can. But we aren't going that way."

Jack frowned. "Then which way—"

"The forest, Jack," Steve said, cutting him off. "We're going through Cran-dor Forest, like your dad and I did."

"What? But you guys went *before* Rancast did his desecration thing, right? No one can go in there after that."

Steve raised his voice and punctuated each word. "There's no other way, Jack."

Jack breathed out a long breath, then nodded. He clutched at the pawn pendant, which had come out from under his torn shirt. "Okay."

"You ready?"

"Yep."

Steve kicked his horse into a gallop, and Jack followed. They raced ahead, dodging explosions and ducking at the constant spraying shots that zipped overhead.

The Thandalians had reorganized in the southwest, on the edge of the high mountains where the Destronn Hollow Road came through. There the soldiers and heroic volunteers were making a stand to protect the retreating masses. Most of the loyal Thandalians now veered that way, and the intense attacks were focused there. What weapons and vehicles the Thandalians had were concentrated there, and they fought back bravely with what looked to Jack like effective results. That lifted his spirits as he thought of Benny and all the terrified civilians in flight.

Jack had slowed, gazing back briefly to try to locate Benny, when a shardhark dove at him, swinging a scything blade at his head. Jack dove off the horse, narrowly avoiding the strike, and landed hard on the packed sand. He sprang up and drew his blade just as the green-black creature came again. Jack hadn't been this close to one since his fight with Mordok. The smell was the same, though this one was darker than Mordok had been. Huge and grotesque, its wings beat wide as its blade came around and it screeched a challenge.

Jack kicked out, but his connecting kick didn't move the monster at all. It was like kicking a wall. The blade came down, and Jack dashed aside, fearing a parry would break his own sword in two. He stabbed out, but the Shardhark blocked this with relative ease, then clobbered Jack with his other hand.

Jack crashed down, losing the grip on his sword. He levered up on an elbow and shook his head clear. Looking up, the shardhark rose into the sky a few yards, then descended on him with his weapon poised.

Jack raised his hands in a futile gesture of defense, but the shardhark was suddenly blown sideways in a blast of orange fire and black smoke. Jack was knocked back by the blast, then gazed through the clearing smoke to see a Thandalian soldier turning his field cannon, mounted on a hill they had just taken, to another target.

Jack pumped his fist as he rose, swung back in the saddle, and urged his horse on through the smoke.

He caught up to Steve, who seemed to have had his own intense battle, and they raced ahead for the distant trees. The closer they got, the farther the worst of the battle was left behind. Both Vandals and Thandalians stayed far away from the forest, even its periphery abandoned by the battling forces.

Jack and Steve rode around a close-quarters battle where the few Thandalians were dramatically outnumbered. Jack focused on their goal: *Michelle*. So he raced on. But Steve did slow. He paused and fired several well-placed shots at the enemy. Then he too wheeled his mount and sped for the trees. Bullets whizzed overhead, and a rocket exploded nearby. But they were through it now. The grave dangers of the war were, for the moment, behind them. Still, Jack felt no relief. Looking back, he saw the inverted star and crown banner, huge and horrible, spread out over the Destrow gate. Rancast's rebels had the city once again—and seemed certain to have the whole world.

The forest loomed before them.

It was thick and dark, with—despite the heat—a kind of low fog oozing from its edges. They rode slower now, approaching with caution.

"We can't talk normally in there," Steve said gravely, "we can only pray. The wood is connected to the power at Andos. It knows things, somehow. I don't understand it, but all we can do is have pure-hearted purpose. So focus on love, Jack. You love Michelle, and I know it. Focus on that love."

"Yes, sir."

"And follow me, Jack, in the rites. They are not against your conscience, believe me. Your father did them with a clear conscience, and so can you."

Jack nodded, Ghistalli's accusation against his father surging up inside his mind. "Wheeler told me." This might be the last chance he'd have to ask Steve about Ghistalli's charge. *Should I ask now? It can't be true.* But he did doubt, because he knew that within him was the hunger for power, the pride of place he battled against so often—the fear of what he might become. Had his own father succumbed to the temptation?

They were at the edge now, and Steve dismounted, placing all his weapons in his baggage on the horse. He led the huge horse in—despite its whining protests. Jack did the same, securing his sword to his saddle and hiding his revolver in among the saddlebags. He followed Steve, leading a reluctant Captain Kirk as they ducked below low limbs and stepped over tangled vines. Then Jack saw something that nearly tore a scream from his throat. He slapped a hand over his mouth as his eyes went wide.

There were piles of skulls and bones just inside the forest. Pyramids of death lay heaped in a warning wall.

Steve grimaced at the sight, then walked on, dragging the frightened horse behind him. Jack followed, forgetting to breathe for a while as his heart pounded.

Once past the heaping wall of death, they quickly came to a beautiful clearing of moss and soft grass. Steve let go of his horse's reins, glanced at Jack, and knelt. Jack imitated him. Bowing their heads, Steve led them in prayer, out loud.

"Our Father, who art in heaven, hallowed be thy name. Thy kingdom come, thy will be done, on Earth as it is in heaven. Give us this day our daily bread, and forgive us our trespasses, as we forgive those who trespass against us. And lead us not into temptation, but deliver us from evil. For thine is the kingdom, and the power, and the glory, forever and ever. Amen."

They remained on their knees, heads bowed, as soft footsteps sounded nearby. Jack closed his eyes tighter, seeing in his mind black-bladed keepers ready to kill. He kept on praying, silently. For his mom. For everyone back home, and for the refugees fighting for their lives nearby. For Benny, Tytrus, and his master, Wheeler. *Oh Lord, please let Wheeler be alive! Please send him to me. We need his sword in Andos. And for Michelle, who only hoped to help her people. Lord, please save her.*

In answer he felt cold steel touching his throat. But he did not move or open his eyes, only prayed on. It seemed a long time later when he finally opened his eyes. He was alive. No forest sprites or menacing defenders stood ready to kill them.

Steve was up and mounted again, a sober expression on his weary face. He motioned his head toward the inner forest.

Jack nodded.

He stroked Captain Kirk, then mounted as quietly as he could, and they rode slowly on, deeper into the forbidden forest. Jack saw green trees and dappled light and heard birds singing the sweetest songs. Tytrus had called the birds doo-wairose. Jack was deeply exhausted. He had been cut in the back, and now his wound ached. He ached all over.

Twice, unable to keep his eyes open, he almost fell from his horse but caught himself at the last moment. Steve was ahead and didn't see, but Jack saw that the older man was sagging in his own saddle.

Jack heard flowing water, and his mind woke somewhat at that sound. He realized he was terribly thirsty. Steve dismounted ahead, and Jack did the same and followed him to the stream.

Steve waved, getting his attention, then pointed to Jack, then himself. Jack nodded. *I understand. I do what you do.*

Steve knelt at the stream's edge, careful not to touch the water with his dirty knees. Jack did the same. Steve rolled up his sleeves slowly, then gently dipped his hands in the cool water. Deliberately, slowly, he washed his hands and lifted the water up his forearms and cleaned them as well. Jack followed his example closely. Finally, after bowing three times, they cupped their hands in the water and drank. Seven times, they dipped and drank, but as Jack bent for an eighth drink, Steve's hand shot out and clasped his wrist. Jack's head swiveled back to Steve; Steve only shook his head slowly, then pointed at Jack, then himself. *You do what I do.*

Steve rose and crossed carefully back to the horses. He led both to the stream and attended to their ceremony himself. The creatures were calm and eager to drink. Jack watched, and, for a moment, he saw across the bank, almost entirely hidden in the trees, an archer all in black. He was sunk in a shadow, disguised and unmoving. It was only a trick of the sun, Jack's eyes going in and out of focus, that allowed the momentary glimpse.

How close was I to dying just for not drinking water right? He shook his head. *No, it wasn't that. It was for not respecting something I don't fully understand, something deeper than I can see right now. How many of those skulls at the forest edge were Ghistalli's soldiers invading this place with bloodstained hands?*

Steve brought back the horses and handed off Kirk's reins to Jack. Then they led them, still on foot, across a small arching bridge. Further into the forest they went, mounting again a few minutes past the bridge.

Jack felt refreshed for a while and shocked awake by the sight of the archer steward, but soon exhaustion dragged at him again.

Steve felt it too, Jack knew, and he turned and motioned for Jack that they would stop there for the night. The horses were left to graze as Jack and Steve grabbed bedrolls and quickly lay down.

Darkness fell over the next hour, and Jack, unable to keep his eyes open, fell asleep to a birdsong of astonishing beauty. His last thought was a pure-hearted prayer.

Deliver us from evil.

Chapter Twenty-Four

Surrender,
or Die

J ack woke in the dead-quiet forest, shaken awake by
strong hands. In his exhaustion, he almost asked Steve
to give him a few more minutes, but his pinched eye
saw another form.

Wheeler!

Jack almost shouted. Almost spoke. But that was against
the laws of the forest, he remembered. And Wheeler had put
his hand over Jack's mouth.

Wheeler smiled and motioned for Jack to follow. He pointed
at Steve, who was awake and packing up the camp in the
predawn. Wheeler, eyes locked with Steve, pointed at Jack
and himself and then to a path. Jack understood it. *I'm showing
Jack something.* Steve understood it too, clearly. He pointed to
himself, then the blankets. He meant, *I'll pack up and meet you
here.* Wheeler nodded and led the way along the path, deeper
into the wood. Jack left his weapons behind, but Wheeler
carried Caladbolg—the Prism Blade—at his side. In the eerie
dimness, the sword glowed faintly.

Wheeler led Jack through uneven moonlight falling on

the forest floor, broken into a thousand pieces by the high trees. They passed a series of moss-covered hovels that almost seemed to merge with the green-grounded mounds rising here and there. In fact, Jack often could not tell what was a hermit's shanty and what was a natural rise in the forest floor. Then he wasn't sure there was a difference at all.

After a long time, Jack saw a basket hanging from a tree before a wide clearing filled with low fog. Jack heard a stream running nearby. Wheeler knelt at the basket, produced a gold coin from his pocket, and placed it inside. He rose and crossed into the clearing, his feet disappearing in the fog. When Jack followed him, Wheeler motioned for the boy to kneel, then flipped him a second coin. Jack caught it, placed it in the basket, and then followed Wheeler into the clearing.

"Well done, Jack," Wheeler said, breaking their absolute silence. Jack's eyes widened and his hands went to his mouth. *Wheeler spoke!* He scanned the trees for archers, expecting a sudden attack from the deadly Stewards of the Black Blade. Wheeler raised a hand for calm. "It is well. Do not fear. I know the ways of Cran-dor Forest. I have traded for a space to speak. And to do more." Jack pointed to himself. Wheeler nodded. "Aye, son. You may speak too."

"Did you just put coins into the forest like a jukebox?" Jack asked.

"I suppose that is a way of seeing it."

"I'm surprised the forest would want money."

Wheeler shook his head. "It is not the money, to be sure. There is no need of money here. It is the giving of something that the giver finds valuable. I value the coins, and so the forest accepts that."

Jack shrugged. "I'm glad you were flush. I don't think I had much to give."

"You will, soon," Wheeler said, his smile disappearing. "I know you have a hard task ahead of you. And I have been thinking of doing this for a long time."

Jack felt a churning in his guts. "*We* have a hard task, right? You're coming with me, right?"

Wheeler drew Caladbolg, and it glowed white above the twisting mist. Wheeler was magnificent then, his eyes shining with the light of the Prism Blade. "This will be yours, Jack, and with it you will ascend the heights of Andos and beyond. You will rise and become more than I ever was."

Jack shook his head and said, "No, it's not time yet," but in his mind the words were different. *It is time. I am ready. Caladbolg is mine.*

Wheeler raised high the blade. "I won this sword when I killed Connelly Redbane, who had, years before, murdered my king. Many have tried to win it from me by combat and killing, but I have held it all these years. And now it comes to you."

Jack bowed his head. "I trust you, Master."

"It begins with kneeling," Wheeler said, and Jack began to drop low, but Wheeler stopped him. "Not you. *I.*" Wheeler closed his eyes and knelt down, fog parting as he descended. He bowed his head low and extended the blade across both open palms of his outstretched hands. "Under the Only God, I hereby surrender Caladbolg, the blade of kings and killers, of legends, Lua's bane, and the strength of Fergus. Surrendered first to blessed Patrick, and in his name, I surrender it now to you." Faint lines of lightning crackled up Wheeler's ankles and then up through his arms to dance along the pale blade.

Jack reached for the hilt and grip, lifting it slowly and raising it high. "I am the master of Caladbolg, the gift of Saturn and prize of Cúchulainn. I am the heir of heroes and kings, and I take this blade to conquer and kill!"

The sword was beautiful, more lovely than any person or thing Jack had ever seen. It fit in his hand like a key to a lock, and the power that surged inside him felt like swallowing the sun.

He gazed down at Wheeler, who now looked feeble and frail. The old man lifted his head, exposing his neck. This was, Jack knew, the end of the ritual. Caladbolg was his now, and he was free—encouraged even, maybe, by the way of the old gods before Patrick—to seal his ownership in blood.

He looked from the pale naked neck of Wheeler to the pale naked blade in his hand. One pulsed with life, and the other was inviting him to end his. He set the ancient blade against his former master's—its former master's—neck. The edge drew blood, and Jack smiled to see it. "Rise!" Jack commanded, pulling the blade away.

Wheeler stood, touching the blood at his neck, a worried expression blooming on his face. "You drew blood in the sacred forest, Jack."

"So what?" Jack looked down at his blade, saw the edge of blood drop from its end and fall, breaking through the fog, to strike the green forest floor.

A note like a gong was heard at that landing, and the edge of the clearing filled with black-robed, black-bladed warriors.

Wheeler stood slowly and staggered back. "What have you done, Jack? What have you done?"

They came then, the dark warriors with flashing swords. In the mist, Jack met them, swinging his blurring blade in bright slashes that cut the legendary warriors down by the score. They came still, on and on, pressing in on him as he wielded his enchanted blade with the power and pride of ancient greats long forgotten.

Finally, after a long—exhilarating, for Jack—combat, it was over. They were all dead. All the defenders the forest had to send were stretched out around the clearing. Huge crows, purple-hued and screeching, circled overhead.

Below, there was only Jack. Only Jack Zulu, the greatest warrior in all the worlds.

Oh, and a sad old man.

Wheeler, aghast at what he had witnessed, fell to his knees, eyes full of tears. "What have you done, Jack? What have you done?"

Jack looked down on him, and the sword caught fire, burning with a blue flame so hot it should have devoured Jack's hand in an instant. But Jack felt no pain, none at all, for what seemed the first time in his life. In place of pain and indecision and his war to hide his pride came a limitless power welling up inside. "I have done what I will do," he said, "and I will do what I have done." Feeling the blade's power coursing through his veins, Jack drove fiery Caladbolg into Wheeler's heart.

And so Joseph Wheeler, sage and scholar, warrior and wiseman, died.

Stepping away grimly, Jack heard the sound of the stream once again. He strode toward it, sheathing the Prism Blade—no longer aflame—as he walked. He was thirsty after all that slaughter and so bent to cup the water in his hands. But he saw that his hands were covered in blood. So he washed them in the water, and, darkened by the polluting red clouds, it took a while to dissipate. When it cleared at last and he bent to drink, he saw his reflection in the clear water. He saw himself.

He saw Rancast.

Chapter Twenty-Five

Prayers
and Pawns

J ack screamed—by the stream or lying down in the forest near Steve, he could not tell—and writhed out of his bedroll. He shook, wiping at his hands as he stumbled to his feet. His hands were red! He knew it was so despite what he saw, and so he desperately wrung them, twisting his grip on his shirt again and again, hoping in vain to rid them of their horrible stain.

Somewhere in the back of his mind, Jack knew he had dreamed it. But he could not tell whether or not what he had dreamed was true. It seemed impossible that he had not killed Wheeler mere moments ago, that he had not seen Rancast in the stream's reflection. It had to have happened. *Had to!*

Even if it were possible—and Jack doubted it was—that Wheeler had not been killed in this forest this night, by his own hand, he was certain Wheeler must be dead. The lingering feeling in his heart was that Wheeler was gone, and nowhere in his imagination was it possible that his master was alive.

He crouched in the deadly silence of the haunted wood. Jack did not move, only wept, straining to gaze through the treetops, hoping to see a solitary star.

Looking over, he saw that Steve was asleep, and somehow his wild convulsions had not wakened the older man. Steve's face was placid as he slept, but tears streamed down his face. Jack wondered what haunted his dreams. *Michelle? Dad?*

It took what felt like hours, but Jack fell asleep again at last. His final thought was that he and Steve were sleeping, exposed in a forest no one in this world would dare to enter for the terror of certain death, and the thing he was most afraid of was himself.

Jack was shaken awake. Steve pointed at his wrist, then the horses. *Time to go.* Jack nodded.

Then the memory of the night's events flooded back.

I killed Wheeler. I killed my master, my friend, the father I needed when my own was gone. Oh, Wheeler. What have I done?

Jack began to cry again, weeping on his knees. Steve was there, and he gripped Jack's shoulders and peered into his eyes. Jack read concern there, but confidence too. In those eyes Jack's reality came more fully back, and he felt that maybe what he'd experienced in the night in this forest wasn't exactly as it had seemed. As it felt. Jack had to believe, against his certain feeling, that what had happened in the vision had not been—true? It was true, he knew that deep down. But what kind of true? It hadn't exactly happened, and that meant something. Still, Jack felt inside as though it had, and in a way he couldn't explain, it really had happened.

Steve motioned to the path ahead, not the side path Jack

had taken in the vision. Steve rolled his hand in a *Let's go* motion. Jack nodded.

It did not take long to pack up. They had no food, so they mounted their horses and rode on. They came to more streams that day, and the first made Jack's heart nearly leap from his chest as he bent to drink in the way he had been shown. Soon it calmed as he gave himself over to the cleansing ritual. Seven times they dipped and drank, now in unison. Jack felt he knew what to do and somewhere along the way had stopped imitating what he saw from Steve and started doing what he knew was right and proper here.

They rose in unison and then watered the horses, who seemed now to know what to do themselves. Crossing another small bridge, they remounted and continued their journey. On and on they rode, till they reached the edge of the forest. Jack was in front now, and he saw the wasteland ahead through the tree line. By instinct he knelt at the forest's border, his head dipping down as Steve joined him on the soft forest floor. Together, they recited the Twenty-Third Psalm.

"The LORD is my shepherd; I shall not want. He maketh me to lie down in green pastures: he leadeth me beside the still waters. He restoreth my soul: he leadeth me in the paths of righteousness for his name's sake. Yea, though I walk through the valley of the shadow of death, I will fear no evil: for thou art with me; thy rod and thy staff they comfort me. Thou preparest a table before me in the presence of mine enemies: thou anointest my head with oil; my cup runneth over. Surely goodness and mercy shall follow me all the days of my life: and I will dwell in the house of the LORD for ever."

After rising, they led their horses out of the forest and into the wasteland and felt the wind again. Jack only now realized that there had been no wind their entire time in the forest. Before them lay a barren stretch of wilderness, with a solitary mountain looming in the distance. Jack felt better, almost well.

The mountain was high, a swirling blur of brown at its bottom and what seemed like snow near the top.

"That's Andos," Steve said, speaking for the first time since they had entered the forest. "Way up top."

"You and Dad went all the way up there?" Jack asked, gawking.

Steve squinted as he gazed up to the top. "I'm not as young as I was when Ruben and I ascended to the top. And we weren't in a hurry then."

The troubling questions—prompted by Ghistalli on the tower—filled Jack's mind. *Was my father a traitor who grabbed the fruit and betrayed his friends?* "Steve? About my dad, is there anything you're not telling me?"

Steve looked down and away, then back at Jack. "Of course. Lots, probably. I've told you what I think you can handle. But there's more. There's always more."

Jack swallowed. "Did Dad take the fruit in Andos? Did he betray you?"

Steve frowned, anger in his eyes. "Listen to me, Jack. Your dad had his faults. We all do. He was a regular guy in lots of ways and far from perfect. But hear me now, son. Ruben Zulu was the best man I ever knew. He was offered an easy way out of the hard things he knew he had to do. And he refused. He fought, and died, defending Michelle—and more than Michelle. He was a hero."

Jack nodded. "I wish I could see him again."

"I see so much of him in you, Jack," Steve said. "You are your father's son."

"Thanks, Steve." Jack replied. He scanned the horizon, wiping at his eyes. "See any sign of the bad guys?"

Steve gazed intently across the plain, then slowly up the mountain. "No, I don't think so. Wish I had my binoculars, but I don't see anything. That means they're either behind us or already on their way up—or, God forbid, at the top. I hope it means we're ahead of them."

"I think the horses are pretty well rested," Jack said.

Steve nodded, and they urged their mounts on. Soon they were racing across the wasteland, eyes thin in the wind as they sped along at a surprising speed. Jack was delighted with his horse, and they seemed to understand each other after so much time together, including the odd experience of the forest. *Attaboy, Captain!*

Steve began to slow his steed as the sun dipped low and they came within a few miles of the base of the mountain. Jack's heart dropped as he gazed at the swirling dust ahead.

Steve swung out of his saddle and patted his Waylander horse. He clicked his tongue at the storm ahead. "It's pretty bad, Jack. I won't lie. And there's no way around it, I don't think. I hope you like sand all up in everywhere, cause that's what's coming tomorrow."

"I love breathing," Jack replied. "Seems off the table up there."

"It's possible," Steve said, removing his blanket and bedroll, "just not convenient."

Jack nodded, making himself a place to bed down. The light was fading. "We can't make a fire, can we?"

Steve shook his head. "Not out here in the open, no. Not with those monsters possibly out there. They're coming. And it'll get cold tonight. Just bundle up as best you can. We'll leave at first light."

"Yes, sir."

They lay still a little while and watched the stars appear. They had grown used to the strange stars of this place on their journey from Gate City and were glad to be seeing them again after their time in Cran-dor Forest.

Steve coughed. "You had a bad dream, Jack?"

"Yes, sir. Real bad."

"Me too."

"Was yours a lie?" Jack asked.

Steve paused a while, then whispered, "I don't know. I sure hope so."

Jack grunted agreement. "Remember when we prayed at the entrance to the forest?"

Steve nodded. "Uh huh."

"Why didn't God answer our prayers?" Jack asked. "Why didn't he deliver us from evil?"

Steve was quiet awhile; then he spoke. "I don't know, Jack. I don't know. Seems like this part of our story is that God is preparing a place for us, but it's in the presence of our enemies. Not their absence. They are here."

"They sure are," Jack agreed.

"But so is he," Steve said. "And he is the Good Shepherd. Your dad believed that."

Jack nodded but was thinking, *and he got killed here*. "Back in Destrow, did you see Wheeler before going to the tower top?" Jack asked.

"Wheeler didn't meet us on schedule. He wasn't there, and Timman—the villain—said we couldn't wait any longer. He said Wheeler would come when he was ready."

"That's not like Wheeler," Jack said.

"No, it isn't. But Timman said we couldn't wait. We had to be on the platform at this specific time. He was acting strange, but he offered to cancel everything—an empty promise, I can see now. Michelle insisted we go. And, reluctantly, I agreed. Neither Captain Bon-hadden nor I were happy with it. But we had taken so many decisions away from Timman—rightly, I see, now—that we felt he deserved to own that part of the process."

Jack sighed. "Looking back, it seems like there were lots of possible traps for Michelle along the way, but Timman didn't get his way. Like the argument over the palace. He was trying to trap her. I still can't believe it."

"Can't believe Timman's betrayal?" Steve asked.

"Yeah. He was my favorite instructor—Michelle's too—at the Gock. I don't know what he could possibly want so much. He killed her. He killed So-addan, his own daughter. Why would he do all that for Rancast?"

"The Enemy wants blood," Steve said. "Look back on history; evil gods have always demanded the blood of children. Sometimes it's for crops, other times for a better career or an easier life, but it's always blood and it's always kids. We do it in our world, too. We just call it by another name."

"It's sickening." Jack spat. "But why did Timman give in to that?"

Steve was silent for a little while. Then he spoke again. "He wants to be a god. Like Rancast. I'm not sure he wants to be Rancast's servant. I think he wants to be his rival."

"So this—this murder and betrayal—is the cost of getting to Andos," Jack asked, "where he can do what Rancast did?"

"Maybe so," Steve answered. "Maybe he got so caught up in his schemes that he had to decide between staying in his role on our side, of being just one good guy among a team, or helping Rancast. Joining up with Rancast—even if he thinks it's only for a time—gave him a chance to fulfill his ambition, to be this super being."

"If your options are all bad, then don't make a play," Jack said, his mind flying back to a flaming Caladbolg in his hands and Wheeler kneeling before him. He drew out his pawn pendant and gazed down at it. "Sometimes the best move on the chess board is not to move at all."

Steve sat up, and his voice was edged with anger. "That's not an option in chess, Jack. And it's not an option in life. Not to act is to act. The world doesn't need more lousy passive men. You've got to *do* if you want to be a man. Make your best move, and live or die by it."

Jack felt those words go to his heart, a heavy blow that wounded him. "I didn't mean to . . ." he began, but his voice trailed off.

"Oh, and one more thing," Steve said, eyes wide in the moonlight, "one more thing—about chess."

"Yes, sir?"

Steve peered down with eyes half-closed in concentration. "No matter what—even if you're just a pawn—you always protect your queen."

Chapter Twenty-Six

A Grim Ascent

J ack woke from a dreamless sleep, one of many to follow over the next several days as they journeyed up the mountain. They made camp in one rough place after another. The dust storm at the mountain's base was a trial, but they made it through to fight their way up the steep trail, gritty from the sand. On the third night, they left the horses, as it had become impossible to go any higher with them.

Jack patted Captain Kirk, rubbing him down one final time. "Go find a good place to graze, boy." The horse nuzzled close, and Jack said goodbye with a tearful eye and a sincere prayer that they would meet again. "I don't want him to get picked up by Ghistalli and used by their army."

"Me either," Steve agreed, unbuckling the last strap on the faithful mustang's harness. "Go on," he said, patting Captain Kirk and his own six-legged steed. They whimpered and trotted off.

By foot, Jack and Steve climbed on, through sometimes perilous passages and up steep inclines. Steve remembered the pathway remarkably well, and that saved them precious time.

Jack followed him, though he sometimes led the way through tangles of thick brush, hacking away with his sword. Steve killed a kind of large deer, which he cleaned and cooked in the mouth of a cave, trying to hide the smoke. Jack learned to clean and prep the skin, using everything possible, considering their haste, from the animal. They did this several times, drying out and preserving the skins, adding them to their bedrolls and blankets for the worst that awaited them above.

They saw no sign of the enemy until the fifth day, when below, in the wasteland, came the torchlights of thousands of Vandal fighters gathering.

"Even if we succeed," Jack said, "they'll be there when we come down."

"One battle at a time," Steve replied, and they went on.

On the sixth day, they came to the snow, and a nearly white-out blizzard almost killed them. Even covered in skins and blankets, with only small slits for his eyes, Jack felt he would freeze to death. The white became so intense that he had to shut his eyes for long periods of time to block out the all-pervasive brightness. Eventually, Jack was only able to go forward by clinging to a strap taken from the horses' harnesses and held in front by Steve as he trudged forward through the thick snow drifts. But they punched through at last, emerging on the eighth day onto the high ridge. Jack could see almost nothing by now, only blurs ahead. He knew something had changed because the temperature had risen significantly and the permanent blur of white had changed to greens and blues.

Steve peeled layers off Jack and urged him to drink. Jack, sweating now but exhausted in a way he had never imagined possible, collapsed.

Later, he did not know how much later, Jack saw two glowing blurry forms approach. He closed his eyes against the pain, then opened them again to see two blurry faces encircled by halos. He felt himself lifted and heard whispered conversation he could not comprehend. And then all was dark.

Jack awoke on a cot in a cozy room, comfortable but for the dull ache in his feet. He heard voices, Steve's and another man's. Blinking, and grateful to be able to see well again, he saw that Steve was sitting by the fire, sipping from a clay mug, while the other man, a bent old man in a heavy robe, stirred a pot over the fire.

"He's strong, though young," Steve was saying. "He'll recover, especially with your treatments from the old gardens. His wound is nearly gone already, as is mine."

"It is not what it once was, but there is healing still here in the ashes. I am glad. For he will have to be strong, if what you say is true," the hunched man said.

"I'm afraid it is," Steve replied, gazing into his cup. "I seem to bring bad news every time I come here. I'm sorry, Hig."

The man—Hig, Steve had called him—smiled. "You tell the truth, Steve. I am grateful for that. I knew this day would come, but I had hoped for more time. While the power of the garden tree is known, villains will try to come and take it."

"How many have come over the years?" Steve asked.

"Not a few," Hig answered, pouring some of the pot's contents—a soup of some kind—into a bowl. "But all died, either in the ascent or trying to get inside. None had the key."

"But Timman does," Steve said, accepting the offered bowl.

Jack thought of calling out, but he felt on the verge of falling asleep again.

Hig went on, dipping more soup into another bowl. "They all attempted the impossible."

"Something about this place and its secrets make people do audacious things."

Hig closed his eyes and sighed. "Ah, yes. Ruben attempted the impossible." Jack's eyes opened, and he was suddenly awake. Hig continued. "It was his brash action that led to the secrets escaping into the worlds."

Jack sat up. "Are you saying it was Dad's fault?" he croaked. "That he tried to steal the secrets of Andos?"

Hig crossed quickly, urging Jack to lie down. The hunched man was very old and scarred, with deep wrinkles surrounding large worried eyes. "Come now, young Jack. Rest. Do not become upset."

"You're blaming my dad!" Jack snapped. "Is it true? Did Steve lie to me?"

Hig frowned. "I don't believe he would."

Steve knelt down by the cot. "There are things I haven't told you, Jack. But everything I told you was true."

"Eat something," Hig said, offering the second bowl of soup to Jack.

Jack accepted it, suddenly ravenous. "Tell me, please," he said, between sips, "what my father did here."

Steve looked at Hig, who nodded. Steve spoke up. "It wasn't my secret to reveal. I told you your father was a hero, and that is true. I told you he protected Michelle and me while we escaped. That's true, but there's more. There were others."

Jack blinked. "Other Thaons?"

"I was one," Hig said, pulling up his shirt and turning to reveal a vicious scar across his upper back. "I will tell you my sad story tomorrow. Rest more tonight. You are weary, Jack. You can rest in knowing your father was a hero whose sacrifice has kept alive the spark of light and hope across the worlds."

Jack did feel exhausted. The bowl, empty now, slid from his grip and fell, breaking on the stone floor. "I'm sorry," he said.

"It is no bother," Hig replied, dipping to pick up the pieces. You rest now, Jack Rubenson Zulu. You do look like your father. Yes, you do."

Jack smiled. "Thank you, Prince Hig."

Hig looked down. "I am a prince no more. I am a Thaon no more. I am but a broken thing," he said, holding out the shards of the destroyed soup bowl. "I was useful once, but my arrogance led me to folly, and I helped lose the world. I grabbed at greatness, and the whole of Thandalia pays for my mistake. I helped Rancast ruin the world."

Chapter Twenty-Seven

The
Lost Thaon

The next day they set off from the village. Jack felt much stronger after a good breakfast and some spectacular tea that would be the envy of any healer in the twelve realms.

The village was small, with fewer than a hundred people living there. It sat on a hillside near the Golden City. Andos, Jack saw in the distance, was imposing up on the summit of the mountain, a city filled with arches and domes, high towers and bridges. Above the city, at its far edge, there was a high spiraling dome.

It took hours to reach the Andos gate. It was broken open and hanging on a rickety hinge. Jack frowned at the dilapidated entryway. Weeds rose to choke the road leading in, with broken bricks scattered along the way. They entered, walking under brown arches, into a dead city. A ruin. A dull gray pervaded, with bland faded brick all over. Jack strained in his mind to see what this could have been before. As they walked in somber silence across a bridge that stretched over a dry riverbed, a sadness welled up within Jack.

Nothing was gold in the Golden City.

"It was not always so," Hig said. "This was as vibrant a life as one can imagine. I played in these streets as a child among hundreds of others. I met Donn just there," he motioned to a dingy cross street where two overlapping arches once converged overhead. "He became my very best friend. We played every day and took our first flights together. His family was Lio-farre, a kind of high order of Thaon. His father was Gate Captain and likely to move on to the Sanctum Guild. Donn was shining in his glory, even among the bright hosts of Andos in that day. He had ideas—beautiful possibilities. His imagination was vast, and I would listen to him plan out innovations that were never revolutionary but always and everywhere undergirded our traditions and history. He was a faithful one, that Donn, but with a heart aflame and a mind like lightning."

Steve put a hand on Hig's shoulder. "I remember him. I wish it had been a longer friendship."

"He would have risen to the place of Arch-Thaon among us," Hig said. "Indeed, he became our last true leader when the elders all fell and we scrambled to answer Rancast's clever devilry."

"He died on the bridge," Steve whispered reverently, "protecting the High Sanctum."

"Yes, he proved his nobility then," Hig said. "*He* would not let them enter a second time."

After a silence, Jack spoke up. "Can you tell me about the High Sanctum?"

Hig pointed to the high spiraling dome on the hill. "The High Sanctum was our life—both Thaons' and the city's. Every year, a representative chosen in our ceremonies would go to the High Sanctum. He would enter and pass, in peace, the guardian of the threshold, whose red sword had for all known time meant certain death to invaders. Then that chosen Thaon would eat from the fruit of the Tree of Light and Hope. When he ate, the healing would renew and all Thaons would rise and fly over the mountain. On the years when it coincided with the festival, we would go out to the Valley of Stars on the eighth day."

"How did Rancast win against the red sword guardian and the Thaons?" Jack asked, his heart heavy. "I know he took the fruit. But how?"

"It was my fault," Hig said. "It is a bitter irony that I am left to tell the tale. A punishment, I suppose. And one I deserve."

"Hig," Steve said, gently chiding.

"You see, Jack," Hig continued, "no one may enter the High Sanctum but a Thaon. It was—and is—impossible to enter as any other unless let in by a Thaon. When Rancast came, I served as his key." He shook his head as tears came. They spilled over his eyes and ran down his scarred wrinkled face. He did not move to wipe them. "I thought that, by my passivity, I could best serve our land and its people. I thought I was clever—that I could match the wit and wisdom of my spectacular friend. I was wrong. Rancast used me as his key, then went to the sacred guardian. I was certain this ancient safeguard would hold and my scheme would be vindicated. I thought I might be celebrated because of it—the savior of Andos." Hig's face twisted in remembered agony, eyes on the High Sanctum above. "But Rancast was not so easily outmatched. By some stolen art, darker than any I had ever heard of, he killed the guardian, and the red sword clanged on the ground. My heart sank for the murder done in that sacred place, but I hoped he would bend to take up the blade and, his heart revealed as what it was, he would die. For the sword is enchanted and is certain doom for any who wield it unworthily. But—wise as a dragon—he left the sword alone and went straight to the fruit. He took it—his greatest prize in all the worlds—and ate. He might have taken the red blade then, but he said he didn't need it. He was strong and no longer simply long-lived. He would now never die of old age. He ate and became more godmonster than ever. Then, in Andos, the opposite of healing happened."

Steve coughed. "You fought him then, Hig. Bravely."

Hig grimaced. "Too late, my action. Too feeble, and too late. He overcame me and cut off my wings, leaving me ruined in a ruined city. But his slaughter had only started, and he murdered scores of my people at once. A war for Andos followed, and we lost more and more every day. Every day until the end."

"Ruben and I came during the war," Steve said, gazing around as they walked on, stepping over rubble. "Wheeler was here too. He fought so bravely, as did Ruben. We helped, but no one could really stand against Rancast. Wheeler fought him and barely came away with his life. After seeing that, I was certain. I don't think any mortal man can really fight him and win."

"Sadly, it is only too true," Hig agreed. "He is beyond defeating by any mortal I have ever known or heard of."

Jack frowned and almost spoke up, but he kept his peace. *I will fight him one day. I will defeat him.*

Steve went on. "With the last remaining faithful few of us—once we knew we were going to lose—a plan was forged. Twelve Thaon babies, all now orphaned by the war, were given to twelve different messengers, each to be taken to the Wayland and then into the twelve realms. Almost no one knew—or knows—about them. They were to be hidden, there in the scattered worlds, until a future time."

"The seeds," Hig said. "And Ruben fought to save them. He died, cut down by Rancast, as he bravely battled to buy the messengers time to get away."

Steve shook his head. "I saw it, with Michelle in my arms. He was . . . glorious. Blazing away with his weapon, he took down many of them. But Rancast was too much. We got away, but Ruben fell there in the street." They had stopped in a square surrounded by half-standing stone buildings, with a ruined fountain at its center.

Hig walked to a spot beside the fountain where the ground was broken. He knelt. "It was here he fell, and here I found him after Rancast had gone on. He was praying, saying 'The LORD is my shepherd.' I held his hand. When he died, I took his gun and his badge, and I buried him below the village. I later sent those items to Steve, along with a letter begging him to stay away from here."

Jack knelt beside Hig. "My father died here, protecting the children—Michelle and the others. He never gave in to Rancast."

"Never," Steve whispered.

Hig rose and stepped back to stand near Steve, head bowed low.

Jack reached out and touched the broken stones beside the fountain. *The stones of my father's blood. My own father.*

"The blood is gone," Hig said, "but not the memory of what he did that day."

"It's not gone," Jack replied in a husky whisper. "It's in me."

He knelt there awhile, remembering everything he could of his father. Finally, he said a prayer for his mother and rose.

Jack stood, rubbing the dust from the street into his palms. "I would have loved to see this square, this city, when it was alive and thriving."

"It was magnificent," Steve said.

"Aye," Hig added. "It was indeed a marvel."

Jack looked around, then up at the spiraling dome on the mountaintop. "When Timman comes, he'll go there?"

Hig nodded. "It won't be easy, but he is familiar with the lore. He will be prepared."

"So all we have to do is stop him," Jack said. "We kill him, rescue Michelle, and prevent another Rancast from plaguing Thandalia and all the worlds."

"Aye," Hig replied. "But he'll have his army along—or some part of it."

"How do we do it?" Jack asked.

Steve scratched his chin. "Ambush, I guess."

Jack nodded. "Tell me what I need to do."

"Let's go to the bridgeway," Steve said, "and we'll get a good look."

"I'll await you here," Hig replied, sitting down on what remained of the fountain's edge. "I need a moment here."

"We'll be back, Hig," Steve said, and he motioned for Jack to follow him. Jack drew alongside Steve, and they left the square, following a winding stone road that ascended gradually toward the High Sanctum.

"He can't bear to go near it?" Jack asked.

"I guess not," Steve replied. "It's understandable."

"He regrets what he did?"

Steve frowned. "I think he more regrets what he didn't do."

"He didn't stop Rancast?"

"He didn't act when the chance was there. He let his pride drive him. I don't speak out of turn. He has said as much to me."

Jack kicked a small stone ahead. "I don't know how a guy's supposed to be in the world. He holds back, and he's wrong. He acts, and he's wrong. He's too strong? Bad. He's too weak? Bad."

Steve shrugged, leading them up a winding road. "It's a conundrum. We gotta somehow stay the right kind of patient and the right kind of active. We gotta be slow to speak but speak up when it's right to. I'm not sure about the right balance in all of life, but I'm sure of one thing."

"What's that?" Jack asked.

"It's time for action, now—for weapons out. Grip 'em and rip 'em."

Jack absently patted his holstered sidearm on his right hip and his sword on his left. "Grip 'em and rip 'em? Is that something you and dad used to say?"

"I think it was your Uncle Freddie's expression. The tomato doesn't fall too far from the tree with those Marinos."

"Uncle Freddie knows how to shoot?" Jack asked. "He never showed Benny how; I know that."

"He showed Benny's older brother—he showed young Fred. Before he went missing. Those two would come to the range with us. Then he stopped doing a lot of things."

Jack nodded. "I guess so. He's still a good dad to Benny and a great uncle to me."

"Just like that, Jack," Steve replied, pointing and shaking his finger. "It seems like a lot of life is what we do with our pain. See, I admire them. The Marinos could have quit. But they keep going. Kept working and stayed together. That didn't involve any weapons or violent battles, but it's braver than people might think."

"Some battles are secret," Jack said, "and don't come with glory."

"But they still save lives and, sometimes, even cities."

They walked on, silent for a while, up the winding, rising street. Blasted-out buildings and half-standing statues lined the way, gray and brown. Dry dirt surrounded the walkways, and Jack imagined it had once held gardens and grass, colorful and glorious. The once-golden city lay in wreck and ruin, and it sickened his soul to see it.

They took a final turn and saw the end of the road up and ahead, wreathed in fog. Steve explained that the mist rose up from a gorge between the city and the High Sanctum. Jack couldn't see anything of the gorge; nor could he see anything beyond the spiral dome. He could see that the High Sanctum above was open in its center. A bridge spanned the gap, thin and once elegant. It was a rope bridge, sturdy and straight, despite its years of neglect. It seemed the world's end was just ahead. Flanking out from the entrance to the bridge lay a walkway and a platform with a high ornate railing along the edge of the gorge.

"We can trap them here," Steve said, motioning toward the heaping weeds on either side of the bridge's entrance. "With some time to prep it, we can have a perfect ambush and get our girl back."

"I'm afraid it's too late for that," came a familiar rasping growl from behind them.

Jack turned, his heart sinking. *Becker Ghistalli.*

Steve swiveled in time to see the blast hit him, a laser-like concussion burst that knocked him back ten feet to skid along the stone road. Jack was close enough so that the blast knocked him down too, but he was on his feet again in a moment. He scrambled to the edge of the foggy gorge as shots rang out behind him.

He chanced a backward glance and saw Michelle, gagged and bound beside Timman, safely far behind Ghistalli and a band of Vandal soldiers. They leveled their weapons and opened fire.

Jack sprang to the top of the stone rail and leapt into the gorge.

Chapter Twenty-Eight

Into the
High Sanctum

J ack fell, blind in the all-pervasive fog, and he wasn't sure he'd ever stop or what he might hit when he did.

It was a tree. Breaking through branches and leaves, snapping as he slowed, Jack struck a thick limb and crashed to a sudden stop. He hung there a little while, dizzy and disoriented. Alarm fading and pain rushing in its place, he tried to inventory his injuries. Some scrapes—possibly even a bad gash or two—and some bruises that would only hurt more and more. But no gunshot wounds.

He was alive and not wounded too badly. He was also up a tree and down a gorge, blind in the mist.

Michelle!

A surging urgency filled him, and he reached out, feeling for his immediate surroundings. Concentrating, breathing deeply and focusing carefully as he reached out feet and hands to find purchase, he slowly made his way down the tree. At the bottom, he felt the drag downward and the angle of the ground. He was on a fairly steep incline, and the rocks he began climbing up made him glad he had landed in the tree.

They were not too difficult to scale as he hurried higher, though he continually reached out, fearful he was taking the wrong way in his ascent. Michelle was in terrible danger. He had no choice but to hurry.

In a few minutes, he had made good progress. Scrambling farther and farther up, he stopped when he heard voices.

I must be near the top.

Straining his ears and slowly creeping closer, he listened.

"When we are over to the other side, destroy the bridge." It was Timman, commanding in his confidence.

"You think there were others with them?" Ghistalli asked in his low menacing tone.

"I leave nothing to chance," Timman replied.

Ghistalli grunted. "That old hunchback is bleeding out in a ditch back there. I haven't seen anyone else since we hit the city. The villagers are pacifists."

"Nothing to chance," Timman said coldly.

"You're the expert here," Ghistalli growled. "But if we cut down this bridge, how will we get back across?"

"I will have powers at that time," Timman said, "that make such obstacles insignificant."

"Don't you mean *we*, Professor?" Ghistalli asked. "We're both eating the fruit. We will be gods, the both of us."

"Of course," Timman said. "But my point is that this will be no great challenge. The important thing now is to get this done without interruption."

"All right," Ghistalli commanded. "Once we're over, cut it down."

Jack heard grunts and shuffling feet.

"I won't help you," Michelle said, and Jack's heart quickened to hear it. She went on. "I don't have the key, and even if I did, I would never give it to you."

"You *are* the key," Timman replied. "Come on."

"Let me help my dad," she begged. Jack could hear that she was crying.

"You can help him once we're done," Timman replied, voice now growing more distant as they started across the bridge. Jack heard the slight strain on the ropes above and to his left. He turned and edged closer in the mist.

"He's dying!" she cried.

"He *will* die, unless you cooperate," Timman said, grunting with the effort of pulling her across. He talked on, but Jack could no longer hear as they crossed toward the High Sanctum.

This was it. The end was here. *Where are you, Wheeler?*

It was now or never, and it was up to him. Both Hig and Steve were incapacitated or dead, and there was no one else coming.

Jack crept close to the edge of the fog, close enough to see the ten or so soldiers gathered near the bridge. Above the fog, Timman dragged Michelle across the stiff rope bridge as Ghistalli sauntered behind them. One of the rebels at the bridge's edge drew out a long curved sword. Steve lay motionless beside the road, two guards looming over him with rifles at the ready.

Too many bad guys. I can't take them all.

Jack crept closer and closer to the Vandals on the bridge, careful to stay concealed in the fog. He crouched down, ears attentive, as the stout rebel began hacking away with his scimitar. Jack edged out of the fog and watched as the man sliced apart the far-side connection of the bridge's ropes with strong overhead strikes. The bridge tottered, uneven, and almost yanked free of its supports on the nearer side. The man smiled and hacked down again, and the bridge hung only by a single rope that frayed quickly in the tension.

Jack dug into a sprint. Surprising the Vandals, he flashed past them just as the last binding cord snapped and the bridge sprang away. Jack darted to the edge, ignoring the shouts from the shocked bandits, and launched into the gorge.

He dove, fully extended, and arrowed into the fog. Hands straining, he sailed through the mist and felt—with a sudden thrill—the rope! Gripping it tight, he reached his other hand up and pulled himself into the frayed end of the bridge as it swept ahead in a rush. He tangled himself in it, awaiting the impact on the other side as the momentum swung the torn bridge across the chasm.

The collision never came. Jack swung out and slowed, drifting back, then back and forth while the motion died down. Surprised, and grateful, he began to climb up. He was hurt, but he did not slow. He ignored the pains as he strained to reach the top.

Jack emerged from the fog and climbed the last bit of the dangling remains of the rope bridge. The lip of the edge on this side of the gorge extended out, Jack saw, realizing why the bridge didn't just crash into the cliffs on this side of the gorge and smash him. Grateful, he gasped for air, breathed in deeply, and staggered to his feet. He winced at the pain in his left leg but ignored it as best he could. Fifty feet ahead there was a golden gate along a high wall, and it was flung open. It glowed, and he ran through it and into the High Sanctum.

He slowed and gazed around in awe. It was a garden, with

the spiral dome tower arching over its center. Beneath that stunning structure there was a tree. The tree was high, with stone steps, or platforms, descending wider and wider as the steps reached down to the floor level. The tree itself was not nearly so big as the tree in the Wayland. It was simple, and the rising steps were surrounded by what must have at one time been a beautiful place. Jack thought of images of cathedrals he had seen, but this was a garden. Or, it had been a garden. It was, like the rest of Andos, ruined. Evidence of violence—no doubt tracing back to Rancast himself—was everywhere. Broken sculptures, a wrecked fountain, shattered benches, and bullet holes pocking the spiral dome above. The tree itself seemed to glow. Were it night, Jack believed it would. He thought he tasted fire in the air here, a certain strange charge that heightened his senses.

Ghistalli finished tying Michelle, arms behind her back and front facing the tree, to a thin pillar near the center steps. Jack glowered at him. Ghistalli's ears were covered with a band of red, and his shoulder bore Rancast's inverted star and crown emblem. He rasped a contemptuous laugh, then crossed to join one-handed Timman, who was kneeling on the threshold of the seven levels of stairs. For there were seven levels of circular stone, rising to the narrowest one at the top, wherein stood the Tree of Light and Hope.

Bones lay across the third step from the top—giant bones laid out in order. Unmoved for many years. *The guardian!* It was him, Jack knew, and for confirmation his great red sword lay near his bony hand.

Timman rose and whispered something to Ghistalli. The warlord's grin faded and he seemed to sober. They took one step up to the first level. Jack knew this was his only chance. He reached for his father's gun.

It wasn't there. Jack's holster was empty.

Chapter Twenty-Nine

The Fire
and the Fruit

Jack gasped. His gun must have fallen into the gorge, lost in one of his wild leaps. He hadn't had time to check for it in his mad dash. Panicked, he reached for his sword.

Still there. He breathed in deep, thrown off by the missing revolver. *I'm too late. I can't take them both. I barely survived fighting Timman, and he was wounded.*

Ahead, Timman and Ghistalli took another step up the sacred stairs of the High Sanctum, nearer the tree whose fruit—Jack now saw, to his surprise—was of varied color. Some were red, others green or blue, and others were golden, still others were purple. Every color seemed to be there.

Jack snuck closer, limping as he came around behind the outside of the tower so that he was closer to Michelle. He couldn't reach her without being seen, but he now heard her struggle to shout despite her gag, as she writhed against her bonds. She knew it was vital that these men never tasted the fruit of Andos. The worlds struggled to stem the threat of Rancast and would be lost if there were three of him—or even two. Thandalia would certainly be lost, and beyond it? Catastrophic woe.

Timman and Ghistalli were on the third step now, and the guardian's bones were near. So, too, the red sword.

"I will take it," Timman said, bending toward the blade.

"Why do you get it?" Ghistalli asked, his gloved hand grasping Timman's robe.

"This is my world," Timman said. "The sword is mine."

"I think not," Ghistalli growled. He seized Timman and threw him back so that he stumbled down two levels.

"Becker, no!" Timman shouted. But Jack saw what Ghistalli didn't—Timman's malevolent grin. Jack remembered Hig's warning about the sword. *Certain doom for any who wield it—unworthily.*

Ghistalli bent and grasped the sword, lifting it in triumph. He inhaled quickly, like a jolt of energy had entered him. He smiled, an ecstatic intensity in his eyes. He shook with the sudden power, and the sword burst into flames. Ghistalli cackled and raised the blade higher. "I am the master! I am the lord of worlds!" He seemed to surge with wild energy, and his eyes were fire-bright. Timman stepped back slowly, his eyes thinning to slits as he watched. Ghistalli swelled, seemed ready to beat his own chest in exhilaration. His proud grin turned then to a grimace. He laughed, gasped a moment, then took three steps sideways, a slight convulsion mixed into his exuberant expression. Then came a short cry and a look of deep shock in his eyes.

Jack watched, his mouth open, as Ghistalli gripped the flaming sword and that fire traveled up his hand and arm, to cross and cover his body in a blazing inferno that finally drew agonizing screams from his tortured face.

"I am the master of worlds!" Ghistalli screamed, refusing to let go of the bewitching blade. With a final cry and a whooshing flare, Becker Ghistalli was reduced to ash, and the red sword, flame gone, clattered to the steps again.

Jack gaped, amazed.

Timman stepped in the smoldering ashes as he ascended, eyes wide and eager. He reached the last platform and neared the tree. Reaching out, he nearly had the fruit in his hand when Jack's blade sped toward Timman's outstretched arm. But he drew it back at the last moment, dodging Jack's strike.

In a flash, Timman's own blade was out as he raked a backhanded slash at Jack, who parried it and staggered down several stairs. Timman looked from the tree to Jack, gauging how much time he had. But Jack limped up several steps and came again, forcing Timman to defend himself.

No matter what, I can't let him take the fruit.

Timman, now fully focused on Jack, fought with determination and passion. Dynamic in his expert attack, Timman drove Jack into immediate and constant defense. Deftly he moved Jack's blade up and down and forced him to move his feet frequently to stay alive. Soon, his mastery paid off as he slashed Jack's sword arm again and again. Pain, hot and searing, ran up his arm. Jack staggered back, then came again, even as he struggled to keep his grip on his blade. A hammering overhead blow that Jack barely blocked was followed by a series of slashes and jabs that had Jack dancing aside, straining the pain in his leg.

Glancing at Michelle, he saw the agony in her eyes as she watched. Tears poured from her eyes. She knew what was happening—what was going to happen.

Jack lunged ahead again, feeling his strength was at an end. Timman blocked Jack's blade, turned it aside, and hammered down, nearly knocking it free from Jack's hand. Jack swiped wildly, forcing Timman to duck. Timman's coat came open as he kicked out, connecting with Jack's bad leg. But Jack had seen what was inside the coat.

A gun.

Hope surged inside as he leapt off his right leg and renewed his attack on the Thandalian traitor. Jack poured the last of his energy into this assault, forcing Timman to defend for a few seconds. Timman was driven ever upward, till he was on the top step, just in front of the tree. Jack feigned a kick, then sliced diagonally across Timman's body. Timman, alert to the deceit, raised his arms and whipped back, unbalanced a moment.

Jack went for the gun.

Diving forward, he lunged and stretched out, fully extended, grasping for the weapon.

He came short and crashed onto the second step. A kick from Timman's boot to his face sent him rolling down the steps, blood running from his nose.

Pain screamed, agonizing and all-pervasive. His body felt broken, and exhaustion clawed at him, melding him to the stone steps, where he was certain he would stay, unable to ever rise.

But he did rise. Bleeding, bone-weary and battered, he rose. He shook his head, blinked away the blurry stars from his vision, and lifted his blade. He stumbled up several steps, swaying as he came.

Jack's eyes rose to meet Timman's, and he prepared for the final fight. Then Jack's eyes fell to Timman's hand.

The Fire and the Fruit

The gun was there. Timman leveled it at Jack and fired.

Jack felt sudden fire in his belly as he was knocked back. He fell hard, crumpling onto the steps and rolling down as his sword slid across the floor.

Shocked and defeated, on the edge of death, Jack watched from the cold stone steps as Timman—child-killer and traitor to Thandalia—picked the sacred fruit and ate.

Chapter Thirty

The
Final Fire

J ack blinked, almost unable to believe what he saw.

Timman was suffused with light. He grew. In the matter of a golden moment, he physically grew taller and stronger. His hand healed and grew again. Jack's life ebbed away on the ground, while Timman transformed into something more glorious than Jack had imagined possible. Light seemed to burst from Timman's skin, and he almost floated. His eyes were bright in a transfixed, transported vision.

Jack saw it all and wept as he lay dying.

"I am the first of a new race!" Timman called, his voice booming through the High Sanctum. "I am a new god and shall recreate this world in my own image. I am The Thandaon! I am eternal!"

Jack gasped for breath, his heart crushed in despair. He strained to see where Timman was going as the transformed villain glided down the steps.

It was to Michelle. He was walking toward Michelle.

"You are, and always will be, the last Thaon, girl," Timman announced, his face bright and menacing. "The new gods replace the old, and as you die, I ascend!"

Michelle was terrified; she seemed to be in an awful internal fight, trying to find her Thaon powers, struggling in vain to transform and take on this usurper. But she sagged in her bonds, weeping. She was as helpless as Jack.

Timman loomed, crackling with murderous intent.

Jack blinked away tears. His focus moved from the pillar where Michelle was bound and powerless to the steps in front of him.

There, a red sword lay.

Jack knew what would happen if he grasped it. Almost certain death if judged unworthy. If judged worthy, then a temptation to power unlike anything he had ever faced or likely had the will to endure. He was certain. He had no doubt. All of his nightmares of becoming like Rancast lay there in that enchanted blade.

Doom. Woe. Ruin.

Either way lay terrible peril.

Glancing over as Timman approached Michelle, he took in a ragged breath and looked again at the sword.

He reached for it, closing the hilt in his hand.

Energy raced into his fist and then his wrist, up his arm, and from there flooded into his entire body. He rose slowly, easily, and a confidence welled inside him, filling him up past his brim, overflowing and overwhelming. Strength and power coursed through him, chasing away his suffering—even as he knew it did not heal his mortal wound. But he felt no pain now. The red blade burst into fire, and Jack felt all the heat with none of the bite. It warmed him deeply and bubbled up inside him like a volcano of raw molten power. Power. Power.

Surging, growing, and overflowing.

The flaming sword was in his hand. The world was there too, he thought, just near enough to grasp. He stepped toward Timman. Michelle saw him. Her eyes were wide and worried.

Timman turned, expectant, and stepped toward Jack. "Die, finally, you troubler of my rise. My last foe, catch fire and die!"

Jack did catch fire then, the flame on the blade breaking out all over him. He knew what this meant, but it didn't faze him just now. He stepped forward, in front of Timman, whose proud smile did not match his concerned eyes. He raised his own blade, his eyes darting to Michelle. Jack knew that Timman would strike at Michelle any moment.

Jack looked back in a sudden glance and saw there the ashes of Ghistalli. Then he turned swiftly again, swinging the fiery sword overhead in a burning blur that scythed through Timman's blocking blade and fell on the transformed traitor with emphatic justice.

Timman, the double-minded man, was finally divided. Dying, he fell on both sides of the pillar where the girl with golden wings was bound.

Jack blazed. He rose higher, feeling a crown of fire on his brow. The power surging inside him now made all his life before this moment feel like a smoky wisp, carried off by the wind. Insignificant. Meaningless. Less than worthy of his care. Jack's mind became a conflagration of powerful certainties.

Now is all. I am now. Now is mine. My fire will never die!

He felt himself becoming invincible, and it was intoxicating. He laughed and squeezed the sword grip tighter. Tighter still. *My power. My hope. My all. I am the crimson blade, and godmonsters fall at my arcing flight!*

Jack raised the blade in triumphant ecstasy. It shot forth a long line of fire, climbing into the sky, blasting open the dome of the High Sanctum. No one had ever done this, he was sure. *I am the great guardian, now. I am the one who was to come. I am the eternal flame!*

Approaching a gate inside his burning mind, past which there was no return, Jack heard something. He turned to see Michelle, still bound but stamping on the floor. Still gagged, this was the only way to get his attention. She stopped stomping and locked eyes with Jack.

And it all changed. The fiery lie that all his life had been nothing until now—that he had been nothing till now—was just that. A lie. In her eyes he saw his life, and everyone he loved, and all who loved him. Mom, Benny, Wheeler, and so many others. And her. She was herself. And that was what Jack loved most.

Jack then did the most ludicrous thing he had ever yet done.

He dropped the sword.

Michelle smiled, and a different kind of tears came to her eyes. Joyful, happy tears, full of love and light.

Jack smiled, then felt again the overpowering agony of his wounds—his mortal wound—and collapsed.

All the fire inside him was gone, but it was clean there, and he was glad. He had acted justly and even—at the last—turned away from the gravest temptation of his life. He could die happy.

I think I will. Jack Zulu closed his eyes.

Chapter Thirty-One

Green
and Gold

J ack *was* dying. He opened his eyes and saw her, free
of her bonds now and striding up the stairs. Golden
wings behind her, she moved with a grave, effortless
grace. Laying hold of the golden fruit, she ate, and the world
changed.

Light spiraled from the tree, and mingled with her light, it
rose in a staggered, swelling band that found the ceiling he had
just destroyed, and the hole was closed again. It was repaired,
better than before his breaking. Jack's gaze dropped, and he
saw the light spilling down the steps, and where it touched
him, he was whole again. Over him it flowed, righting his
injured leg and healing even his fatal wound. He inhaled a
full, refreshing breath and stood up.

Michelle descended the stairs and took his hand, and he
felt there a warmth more modest than the red sword's fire, but
he wanted this far more. This was the unmistakable touch of
love and had in it no self-destructive pride.

They walked along the band of light as it grew and flowed
out. Jack didn't know if they followed it or if she was making

it, but he walked on, his heart beating with a growing hope. The High Sanctum grew deeply green, with flowers blooming and fruits bending the branches of healthy trees. And there was water. It surged up from somewhere—Jack didn't know where—and flowed through the garden in a hundred streams leading to one river in its center.

They walked on, out of the High Sanctum and onto the restored rope bridge, which rose and reassembled even as they stepped onto it. Now the reanimating power raced ahead, and Jack saw the rebel bandits fleeing in the distance. The brightness reached the far side of the gorge, sweeping away the fog and revealing a scene of multicolored trees, like Myrtle in the fall. And there, waiting for them at the end of the bridge, was Steve. He was standing, grinning and flabbergasted, healed, with hands held out in awe.

Michelle turned to Jack and smiled, then let go of his hand and ran to hug her father. Despite her glory, bright wings and all, she was swallowed up in a spinning embrace that drew tears again from Jack's eyes.

Then they walked on, the three of them, as the city burst alive with streams running, and green growing, and the golden city gleaming in the sunlight. Andos was becoming again what it had been before Rancast's abominable acts. It was remembering. It was coming back to life. And the Thaon girl, each hand holding an outworlder she loved, walked through the middle of the golden city.

"You did it," Jack said, smiling over at Michelle. "You transformed into a Thaon again."

"I didn't transform," she replied, though kindly. "This is me. This is a capacity I have, not something I sometimes become or pretend to be. I am a Thaon, always, and always Michelle."

"How did you get through the block?" Steve asked. "How did you—I don't know—access your Thaon side again?"

"It was seeing Jack," she said, turning back to him. "It was seeing you lay down the red sword. I knew, somehow, what that cost you and how hard it was. And it was gratitude, and love. It was love that broke the block that kept me from walking into this capacity—this part of me. I had tried many times with anger, with hatred and with fear—even today I tried that. But this is a gift of love, and I cannot give it without love."

"And it is a lovely gift you're giving," Steve said, pointing at a newly sprung cataract racing down into a river in the distance. Green was everywhere, and gold alongside.

"It's not me, really," she replied, smiling wide. "It's a feast I just showed up to. I showed up to serve. I didn't make the feast."

Jack nodded to Steve. "In the presence of mine enemies."

Steve smiled. "Baby, don't you have some duties? Aren't the Thaons supposed to swoop out over the mountain or something?"

"Yes, you're right, Daddy," Michelle replied. "I wish I wasn't alone in doing it, but I am very glad to have the chance to witness this renewal."

"You won't be alone," they heard. They turned to see Hig, wings beating in the violet sky behind him, healed and whole and magnificent in his golden glory. "We will go together, Michelle."

Michelle's mouth fell open, and grateful tears pooled in her eyes again. "I'm not the last Thaon," she whispered. Michelle hugged her father, then Jack. Then she leapt up, beating her wings to join Hig in the sky. They raced aloft and arced over the city, synchronized in a mesmerizing flight that reached to the edges of Andos. Everywhere they went, the curse receded, and the healing took hold.

After a little while, the two Thaons landed, and they all embraced again.

"Baby, I know you didn't go all the way around the mountaintop yet," Steve said. "I watched you most of the time you were up there."

"No, Daddy," Michelle replied. "I asked my elder if we could say goodbye again. I think we have farther to go."

Hig nodded. Jack couldn't get over the change in him. No longer hunched over and wounded, he was strong and extraordinary. Jack felt he ought to kneel. "There is trouble in the wasteland," Hig said, "at the base of the mountain. A battle. We will go there. We may be some time."

"If there is a fight," Michelle said, her face serious, "then I want to go help. We have lost so much."

"We'll meet you down there," Steve said, looking over at Jack, who nodded. Steve went on. "Jack and I will take the ground route, which will take a little longer, but we'll get going as soon as we can and aim to meet you there."

"Be careful," Michelle said, hugging them both again.

"You be careful," Steve said, giving her one last squeeze. "I'm a grown man, and you're the one flying all over the place. I'll be fine. Plus I've got a Mr. Zulu by my side, coming out of Andos alive after a victory over the bad guys." He looked around the mountain city, lush with green, bright with gold, and flowing with crystal water. "I'm on top of the world."

Chapter Thirty-Two

Falling Action

J ack laid a colorful bouquet at his father's grave, and Steve did the same.

They had picked the flowers from the endless variety blooming in and around the golden city. These had mostly come from the blossoming garden surrounding the village's ring of glory, where Ruben Zulu's statue had stood for many years. The ring was a few miles walk from Hig's house, and it was a few more miles to the graveyard. This cemetery was simple and similar to ones Jack had known back home. The gravestones weren't upright here but laid longwise over the resting places and inscribed, often with a picture etched. Ruben's had no image etched, though Jack and Steve agreed that the ring of glory statue was a remarkable likeness. Here there were only words below a simple cross.

Ruben Mduduzi Zulu 1945—1973
Husband ~ Father ~ Friend
A Faithful Man and a Hero
1 Corinthians 15:20-26

After paying their respects, which included repeating the Twenty-Third Psalm, they knelt and prayed. Jack thanked God for his father—for who he was and for what he did. With tears in their eyes and gratitude in their hearts, they left.

In the afternoon, Jack spent an hour in the ravine looking for his father's revolver. He was afraid it had been transformed or destroyed in the remade glory of the new Andos. But he found it, loaded it, and returned it to the holster at his side. His sword still swung at his left side. *One day these will all be laid down. But for me, not yet.*

That evening they packed. They took all the supplies they needed from Hig's house, knowing that the journey would be dangerous and that Hig would be happy for them to have what they needed. Jack found a bright red hat that he felt would work for both the snow and the sand. The next morning, they set off on their return journey. It took them several days to descend the mountain, but it was much easier and quicker than their ascent.

Halfway down, they could see a large band gathered in what had been the wasteland below, but now was green with a great river running through it. The people were camped near the river, between the mountain and Cran-dor Forest. Neither Steve nor Jack were alarmed. They carried on.

Not long after, they emerged from the sandstorm—as strong as it had been on their ascent—and walked toward the camp as the sun set in the purple evening sky. They saw a banner waving in the gentle wind. It was Rancast's banner, his inverted star and crown emblem, but this had been painted over with a big red X. The Thandalian flag flew above it.

They walked on, and Jack smelled something cooking.

He was delighted to find Benny at a grill, serving hot food for what was clearly the Thandalian loyalist army.

Benny turned around, and his mouth fell open. He tossed his spatula away and ran for Jack, leaping into his arms. "Jack is back!"

"I'm so glad to see you, B!" Jack said, tackling his friend to the ground.

That drew attention, and soon a crowd was gathered around the two weary but happy mountaineers.

Tytrus ran over and jumped on the dogpile. "We heard what you did up there, Jack! It's amazing! Everything's turned around."

Then Michelle appeared, running through the parting crowd to hug her father, then Jack, as he got to his feet again. Behind her, walking their way, came Hig. Alongside the Thaon walked Joseph Wheeler.

Jack hugged Wheeler. "I'm so glad to see you! I was so worried about you."

Wheeler grinned. "I believe that is my line, Jack." He laughed and pulled Jack in for another hug. "It is wonderful to see you, son. I am so proud of you. I know what you did, and it is a thing for which to give thanks."

"Amen," Steve agreed, reaching to shake Wheeler's hand. "Good to see you, Joe."

Hig bowed to Steve and Jack, and they returned the bow. Jack realized, then, that both Thaons were wingless. You could, of course, tell there was something special about them—and Hig was vastly different than when Jack had first seen him—but they blended in well with the jubilant Thandalians all around.

"What happened here?" Jack asked.

"Oh, buddy," Benny replied, "it was some war, dude. The loyalists all regrouped by Destronn Hollow, like when you guys split, remember, and it was preeeeetty bad times. But we all regrouped and fought back, and hey, we're made of some stern stuff, us Thandalian loyalists. So when the bulk of Rancast's goons—after they had secured the city again—took off around the forest, headed here, we were like, 'Let's go get 'em and fight 'em.'"

Tytrus grimaced. "Specifically, Sage Wheeler arrived, having escaped Timman's trap, and he led a volunteer party to pursue the Vandal rebels."

Wheeler looked over at Michelle. "We hoped to rescue the princess or to do anything to slow them down."

Benny nodded. "Yeah, and we caught up with them here. The main baddies had already gone up the mountain with Michelle to face off with you guys, but we laid into the rest of 'em, even though we were outnumbered by a ton."

"And, even though we were outnumbered," Tytrus went on, "we still . . ."

Benny continued. "We still . . . got whooped real bad. And we kept getting whooped for two days. It was really bad down here."

"That is, until the third day," Tytrus said. "Everything changed that day."

"Yeah," Benny went on. "There was this sudden rush from above. The light changed, I think, and the river filled again. That really did a number on the enemy's position. Their camp was in the riverbed, and they got wrecked. It was awesome!"

"Many odd things occurred then," Wheeler said, "and there will be stories of what happened coming to us for many years.

But we do know that the wasteland changed and that our side was reinvigorated by the river and what it did. Then from the forest, which we had carefully avoided, issued forth a band of black-clad warriors who rushed out and joined our side in the fight. Their archers were expert, and their black blades fairly sang as they sailed into the thick of the battle."

"I think they turned the tide," Benny said, pumping his fist, "and we started winning. But it was over—I'm telling you, *over* and done with—when Michelle and Hig swooped down. Mama mia, you have never seen a retreat like that!"

"They ran away, the Vandals, anywhere they could flee," Tytrus said. "Many surrendered. Some tried to go into the storm and up the mountain, and others tried to go back the way they came. Some fools ran into the forest! That was not a good decision, I'd wager."

Wheeler shook his head. "No doubt they regretted it."

"Then it was all over," Benny said. "We had lots of wounded, and Michelle jumped right in, doing her thing, helping care for everyone who was hurt. Turns out, Hig ain't no slouch at that either."

"I know," Jack said, smiling at Hig.

Hig smiled back, nodded, then frowned at Jack. "By chance, is that my red hat?"

Jack grinned. "Yes, sorry. We kind of looted your house."

Hig laughed and snorted as he grabbed his belly while Jack passed over the hat.

"Hig, one thing about ol' Jack," Benny said, shaking his head, "is, yeah, he's kind of a hero, and he does all this legendary stuff. *But*, and it's a big but, he'll take a dude's hat." Benny held up his hands. "Picture this. Fourth grade. Field trip to the state capitol in Charleston. I'm loving life because I've got my new WVU hat on, and I'm certain the ladies are admiring it. Side note: This is before I got my beloved Myrtle Cardinals hat from my big bro. Anyway, Jack compliments it right away. 'Nice hat, B,' he says. So there's your motive right there. Wouldn't you know it, it turns up missing. I'm tuned into it right—"

"Benny," Michelle interrupted, "maybe this isn't the time?"

"If not now, when?" Benny asked. "What could possibly be more appropriate right now?"

Jack hooked an arm around Benny and guided him back toward the camp. "How about you get back on the grill and make me something to eat? I'm starving."

On their way, they passed a small corral, and Jack stopped. "Is that . . . ?" He ran over and wrapped his arms around a beautiful golden horse with a black muzzle. "Captain Kirk!"

Chapter Thirty-Three

Jack to Earth?

A week later, Jack mounted Captain Kirk as their now-diminished crew headed off with aims of making it to Gate City, then to the Wayland, then home to Myrtle. They said goodbye to Hig and many other friends, promising to return again when they could. Hig and Michelle had spent many days together, and Michelle told Jack that what he shared had meant the world to her, enlightening her to her people's history and ways. Jack was glad and was sorry himself to say goodbye to his Thaon friend. Most of the army left on a mission to retake Destrow, which Wheeler believed they would accomplish. Wheeler, along with Tytrus, Steve, Jack, and Benny, accompanied Michelle.

The journey to Gate City took weeks, but it was a joy to see the changes beginning to take hold all over Thandalia. Taking the Highway of Light, they eventually passed the famous Gatton Bridge over a raging Talvar River.

Michelle insisted that they stop at Freston Village again, the once burned-out place they had visited on their way to Destrow. The restored bell rang out as they entered. Like they had seen in many other places, Freston flew the inverted star and crown emblem, crossed out with a red X, below the Thandalian banner. Wheeler smiled at seeing it. "Oh, yes. Thus always to Rancast."

There in Freston they received news that the loyalist army had liberated Destrow once again and that every major city was now firmly held by faithful Thandalians. Freston took that news and Michelle's visit as a double cause for celebration. The travelers stayed there two days and were treated like conquering heroes—which they were.

Dunny was there, the little Freston boy they had first met as a refugee in Gate City. He was thrilled at their coming and introduced them to his mother. They stayed at his house, which was modest and lovely. Having Michelle stay there was the honor of a lifetime for their family, and Dunny was heard boasting to the other children that the princess was his particular friend and relied on him for advice. Jack taught him how to sword fight with some sticks, and Benny gave him a 1984 Cincinnati Reds outfielder Dave Parker baseball card that had somehow survived the journey in his jean jacket pocket.

They left Freston amid cheers and tears from the villagers. Taking the path between the Brothers, those gigantic rocks that hid inside them the ancient ruins of Balmard, they hurried on to the last stage of their journey. Finally, they made their way down into the canyon and on to Gate City as the sunset loomed.

Gate City was nearly deserted, as many of the refugees there had gone home or were on their way home. Those with Thandalian horses left them in the corral; then they all walked toward the gate tree, each one stretching as they went. Jack dismounted but led Captain Kirk by the reins.

"How different everything is now," Wheeler said.

Michelle beamed. "I can't wait to share the news with our Thandalian community in the Wayland. They will be flocking back here, helping rebuild this beautiful world. And they will need so much help."

"It's true," Steve said, "but you also need some rest."

"Oh, believe me, Daddy," she replied, "all I want now is to go home, hug Mommy and my brothers, then sleep for a week."

Steve nodded. "Me too, Baby."

Jack smiled, thinking of his mother and how happy they would both be to see each other again. "Sure, reuniting with family is great, but I could really go for some pizza."

Benny nodded. "Free pizza on me. It's the least we Marinos can do for all you world-savers. And believe me, I am committed to doing the very least I can."

"Pizza sounds perfect," Wheeler said, drawing the gate key from an inner pocket. "And I could certainly obliterate some orange and grape pop right about now."

Benny shot a thumbs-up. "All the grorange pop you can drink, Master Wheeler. Coming right up."

Jack looked over at Michelle and saw she was looking at him. He smiled, and she smiled back, then looked away. Jack's heart felt warm, and he handed Captain Kirk's reins to Benny with a subtle, significant look. Benny took them in one hand, the other darting to his mouth to hide a smile.

Jack hung back as Wheeler inserted the key and whispered the words, and the gate in the center of the tree glowed and opened. Wheeler bowed to Steve, who led the way in, followed by Tytrus, then Benny and Captain Kirk. Wheeler bowed to Jack and Michelle, who came last, but Jack motioned for Wheeler to go ahead.

"After you, sir," Jack said.

Wheeler glanced from Jack to Michelle, then back. "Oh, yes. Of course. Very good." He crossed into the Wayland.

Jack and Michelle stood side by side, looking together at the threshold of another world. They turned in the gateway then, facing one another, as white flakes drifted through the passageway and swirled around them.

"I love it here," Jack whispered. His heart beat loud as he gazed into Michelle's eyes and reached for her hands. She reached out too, and their hands met and twined together. At that touch Jack felt an electricity unlike anything he had so far known. She smiled, and it seemed like she felt the same. Jack bent forward but was interrupted by a voice from the gateway.

"Jack, get in here." It was Benny.

A crease appeared on Michelle's forehead, and they turned and, hand in hand, crossed into the Wayland.

Jack immediately remembered how they had to adjust to the difference of the sun in Thandalia—how it took them a while to see properly. It was like that now, but instead of a brightness, Jack's eyes adjusted to a blurry gloom of the sunset. Letting go of Michelle's hand, he rubbed at his eyes. The white flakes danced all around, but an acrid smell filled the air. Jack blinked away the blur and gazed, open mouthed, at the Wayland at dusk.

The white flakes swirling were ashes, polluting the sky from a fire in the distance.

"It is the Great Tree," Wheeler said, his broken voice breaking the stunned silence. "It is . . . oh, my . . . it's burning."

Gray smoke swirled in the distance, and the blue tower seemed surrounded by a black mist. But, blinking again, Jack's vision cleared and he saw that it was no mist. It was crows, thousands of huge black crows, flying in a mass around the tower. Scanning the skies all around, he saw more crows, their screeches carrying on the evening breeze. Then, there above the Thandalian refugee camp, half-shrouded in the billowing smoke from the burning tree, flew scores of shardharks—the mothmen of Kaalgrad. Michelle pointed to the top of their school, the Gock, where a new flag was flying high over the Wayland—an inverted star with a three-pronged crown above it.

"Oh no," Wheeler said.

The End.

A preview of

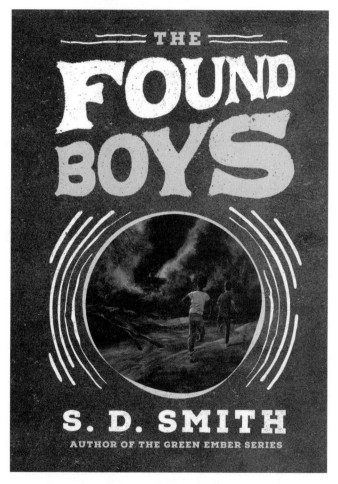

THE

FOUND BOYS

S. D. SMITH

AUTHOR OF THE GREEN EMBER SERIES

Available
September 2024

CHAPTER
ONE

You can learn a lot by a man's handshake—first, for instance, that he has a hand. Second, that he has a skill shared with our friends in the dog world—the ability to shake. Third, that he's a fool for trusting his precious human hand to the megaton squeezing power of mine.

"Ow!" said Tommy Tucker, two years my junior.

"Sorry, Tommy," I replied with deeply sincere concern. "Sometimes I forget how incredibly strong I am."

Tommy stuck out his tongue and rushed out the wide church doors. While our fathers, suit-clad and chatty, discussed the sermon, I chased after Tommy as he fled for the swings over the hill behind the old church.

The swings sat across from the new shelter where we had cookouts. Horseshoe pits and

a rotting volleyball net were crammed near the shelter to leave space for the softball field. Behind the field? You want to know what was behind the field? Woods and water. An explorer's paradise.

"Tommy, you ignorant Philistine," I yelled patiently, "wait for me!"

"You're too slow!" he shouted back, much like Goliath might have shouted at the hosts of Israel. He sped ahead.

Now, I wasn't slow. I was just careful. I prided myself on my ability to outthink the opposition and swiftly arrive at conclusions by means of my brain. I would always win because I didn't need to outrun anyone; I could outsmart them. I thought about my brainpower as Tommy Tucker's form grew smaller in the distance.

When I caught up to him, Tommy was slumped into the seat of the best swing, pretending to sleep.

I frowned. "You took the best swing again."

Tommy pretended to wake up, yawning widely as he tried to hide his smile. "Oh, hello, Scott. I got tired of waiting for you and took a little nap here on Old Number One." He rattled the swing's chain and grinned. "The rocket launcher."

"You always get the rocket launcher," I said, not whining for sure.

"To the victim goes the spoiled."

I rolled my eyes. "It's 'to the victor go the spoils.'"

"Nuh-uh," he said, leaning into a deep pump to get the rocket launcher fired up. In a few moments, he was soaring high and smiling wide, like a spoiled victim of too much speed.

I started pumping my legs—tightly tucked in on retreat, extended like two jutting javelins on outswing—and tried to catch up to Tommy's dizzying heights.

I rose higher and higher, side-eyeing Tommy all the while, as the foundations of the swing set shook and the rhythmic *ding* of chain on aluminum provided the only percussion to ever come this close to Valley Baptist Church.

Then Tommy flew.

He sailed free of the swing, arms flailing and

wild joy on his face. It was a dirty trick, launching without any warning. Everyone knows the rules. You don't just launch without an announcement. But he was intent on depriving me of the rocket launcher. *Not today, Tommy!*

Instead of launching in turn, I dug the heels of my wingtips into the dirt and slipped off my swing just as Tommy was turning to race back and reclaim Old Number One. Ignoring the mom-defying dirt on my wingtips, eyes wide to spy out Tommy's progress, I stepped sideways to secure my prize. Seeing that Tommy was well behind me, I spun to grab the swing. I had failed, however, to properly calculate the trajectory of the rocket launcher. It rocket-launched into my face, slapping me with the faded plastic seat, then following up with a flailing beatdown by chain. I reeled, of course. It was the only thing possible to do. Any boy would have reeled, and I did reel. Spinning away, I struck my head on the swing's A-frame pole and slumped to the ground.

Tommy was very concerned and inquired if I was okay from the comfort of his seat on Old Number One.

"I'm fine," I said, feeling the knot form on my head through my hair. "I was just checking out the grass. It's very short, I find. Must have got a trim."

"Do you have a concussion?" Tommy asked.

"Yeah," I replied, not wanting him to know that I had no idea what a concussion was. "My dad got me one."

"No he never," Tommy said. "A concussion is when you bang your brain and you go stupid for a while."

"Nah." I rubbed my head some more, then spit enthusiastically. "Stupid isn't in my vocabulary. It's just a stinger. Let's go to the creek."

Tommy nodded, then frowned and scowled at me. "You trickin' me so you can get the rocket launcher?"

"Nope," I said, though now that he mentioned it, it was a great idea.

"You swear?"

"Not allowed," I said, pointing to the church. "But I give you my word." I spit in my hand and held it out to Tommy. He nodded, solemnly spit into his, and our hands squished together in a human-to-human shake. I preferred the human shake, as I had been secretly terrified of dogs since forever. One minute they are shaking your hand, and the next they are biting it off. You can't trust them. In my book, dogs are man's best enemy. The wizard up the creek had dogs. I thought about the pearl he stole, and a thrilling shiver of fear jolted through me.

Me and Tommy sprinted for the creek, and I glanced back up at the church as we ran. My parents were outside in the parking lot now, still talking away. I had an eerie feeling I might not ever see them again.

**Order *The Found Boys*
at Christianbook.com,
Amazon.com, or wherever
fine books are sold.**

Keep up with Author S. D. Smith

To get the latest news,
sign up for S. D. Smith's newsletter
and receive a free audiobook!

sdsmith.com/updates

This is the place we share news first, including any deals or giveaways we have available. It often includes some humor and always an honest invitation into this adventure we're on of sharing stories with kids–new stories with an old soul.

If you loved Jack Zulu 1 & 2 hit us with
your own 5 Star Review!
Amazon   Goodreads   Audible
Thank you so much!